The Redheaded
Outfield

and Other Baseball Stories

The Redheaded Outfield

Outfield

and Other Baseball Stories

ZANE GREY

GRAMERCY BOOKS
New York • Avenel

This edition is published by Gramercy Books,
distributed by Random House Value Publishing, Inc.,
40 Engelhard Avenue, Avenel, New Jersey 07001.

Random House
New York • Toronto • London • Sydney • Auckland

Printed and bound in the United States of America

Library of Congress Cataloging-in-Publication Data
Grey, Zane, 1872–1939.
    The redheaded outfield and other baseball stories / Zane Grey.
      p.   cm.
    ISBN 0-517-12423-8
    1. Baseball stories, American.   I. Title.
PS3513.R6545A6   1995
813'.52—dc20   95-32410
                                                                        CIP

8   7   6   5   4   3   2   1

Contents

Introduction

WHILE best known for the Western novels that, at the height of his career, made him the best-selling novelist of his time, Zane Grey (1875–1939) also wrote prolifically about one of the other great passions of his life: baseball.

A talented ballplayer in his youth, Grey chose from among a number of scholarship offers and enrolled at the University of Pennsylvania. There he was prized as both a pitcher and a slugger and seemed destined for a career in the majors. Midway through his college ball career, however, the major leagues moved the pitcher's mound ten feet farther from home plate. This change in the game's geometry proved the undoing of Grey's finely honed pitching skills, and ended his hopes of making the big leagues.

Though not able to make a career for himself in professional baseball, Grey kept a lifelong love of the game alive by following the semipro career of his brother and, when he turned to novel writing, by bringing his fiction-writing talents to the game he loved so well.

While never critically acclaimed as a literary stylist, Grey's immense success and lasting popularity as a

Western novelist are grounded in his raw storytelling power, his vivid description, his swift-paced plotting, his enduring morality-tale themes, and the warmth and appeal of his characters. All these virtues are evident in this collection. Here, too, are a few surprises for the reader of Grey's Western fiction, for Grey's baseball stories have a rich vein of wit and humor not consistently found in his other work.

Grey's gift for description is clearly evident in his depiction of the colorful world of minor-league baseball. Just as Grey's frontier novels brought the Old West vividly to life, the stories in this volume evoke a vanished, more innocent period in both our national history and our national pastime. The oddball collection of players and coaches—the country-boy phenomenons, the wised-up veterans, the obsessed fans, the conniving owners—spring to life as they come together for a summer ritual in the ballparks of small towns and cities dotting the country.

In the title story, "The Redheaded Outfield," a minor-league manager in the thick of a tight, late-season pennant race must cope with a wildly eccentric trio of outfielders. Too talented to bench, too unpredictable for a manager's peace of mind, Red Gilbat, Reddy Clammer, and Reddie Ray are three unforgettable characters. The tale's sharp suspense derives not only from the always unpredictable nature of baseball, but also from the erratic behavior of the weird and wonderful characters who play the game.

The cycle of stories starting with "The Rube" is the centerpiece of this collection, and it displays the full range of Grey's storytelling talents. The Rube, a.k.a. Whitaker Hurtle, is discovered by a hungry manager foraging in the bush leagues for a pitcher that could take his team to the championship. Snapping up the lanky hurler, the manager finds he has an enormously talented—and enormously temperamental—player on his hands. With a pitching repertoire that includes an "unhittable" drop and a vicious beanball, the Rube challenges manager Connelly's skills not only as a baseball coach and strategist, but also as amateur psychologist, matchmaker, and touchingly, surrogate father.

The Rube's progression from rawboned, bumpkin hurler to accomplished professional big-leaguer is detailed in stories that range from the suspenseful and the moving to the riotous. "The Rube's Honeymoon," in which the Rube brings his new bride on an extended road trip with his team, is pure hilarity, as the rough-edged ballplayers are mystified, inspired to spectacularly cruel practical jokes, and ultimately, awed by the presence of Cupid in their midst.

"The Knocker" is a short tale that, in a few strokes, paints a vivid portrait of a character type all too familiar to the fan of today's game.

"The Manager of Madden's Hill" and "Old Well-Well" are two bittersweet stories exploring the game's powerful appeal to a young, handicapped boy and an elderly man. These well-crafted stories display Grey's compassion while never lapsing into sentimentality.

Above all, these stories are pure baseball. Grey's love of the game is manifest in every scene, as is his understanding of baseball's complexities and subtleties. Readers encountering Grey's depiction of a battle between a pitcher on the mound and the hitter at the plate won't fail to see that they are in the hands of a master storyteller who has a veteran's view of the game.

It was a fortuitous convergence of talents in the person of Zane Grey that made these stories possible. Baseball, like the frontier, has an enduring fascination for us. How fortunate that one of our most popular, best-loved authors has given us stories and novels of both worlds that are as fresh and entertaining as they were when they delighted readers more than a half century ago.

MICHAEL BRADLEY

New York
1996

The Redheaded Outfield

and Other Baseball Stories

The Redheaded Outfield

```
○
```

THERE was Delaney's red-haired trio—Red Gilbat, left fielder; Reddy Clammer, right fielder, and Reddie Ray, center fielder, composing the most remarkable out-field ever developed in minor league baseball. It was Delaney's pride, as it was also his trouble.

Red Gilbat was nutty—and his batting average was .371. Any student of baseball could weigh these two facts against each other and understand something of Delaney's trouble. It was not possible to camp on Red Gilbat's trail. The man was a jack-o'-lantern, a will-o'-the-wisp, a weird, long-legged, long-armed, red-haired illusive phantom. When the gong rang at the ball grounds there were ten chances to one that Red would not be present. He had been discovered with small boys peeping through knot-holes at the vacant left field he was supposed to inhabit during play.

Of course what Red did off the ball grounds was not so important as what he did on. And there was absolutely no telling what under the sun he might do then except once out of every three times at bat he could be counted on to knock the cover off the ball.

Reddy Clammer was a grandstand player—the kind

all managers hated—and he was hitting .305. He made circus catches, circus stops, circus throws, circus steals— but particularly circus catches. That is to say, he made easy plays appear difficult. He was always strutting, posing, talking, arguing, quarreling—when he was not engaged in making a grandstand play. Reddy Clammer used every possible incident and artifice to bring himself into the limelight.

Reddie Ray had been the intercollegiate champion in the sprints and a famous college ball player. After a few months of professional ball he was hitting over .400 and leading the league both at bat and on the bases. It was a beautiful and a thrilling sight to see him run. He was so quick to start, so marvelously swift, so keen of judgment, that neither Delaney nor any player could ever tell the hit that he was not going to get. That was why Reddie Ray was a whole game in himself.

Delaney's Rochester Stars and the Providence Grays were tied for first place. Of the present series each team had won a game. Rivalry had always been keen, and as the teams were about to enter the long homestretch for the pennant there was battle in the New England air.

The September day was perfect. The stands were half full and the bleachers packed with a white-sleeved mass. And the field was beautifully level and green. The Grays were practicing and the Stars were on their bench.

"We're up against it," Delaney was saying. "This new umpire, Fuller, hasn't got it in for us. Oh, no, not at all! Believe me, he's a robber. But Scott is pitchin' well. Won his last three games. He'll bother 'em. And the three Reds have broken loose. They're on the rampage. They'll burn up this place today."

Somebody noted the absence of Gilbat.

Delaney gave a sudden start. "Why, Gil was here," he said slowly. "Lord! He's about due for a nutty stunt."

Whereupon Delaney sent boys and players scurrying

about to find Gilbat, and Delaney went himself to ask the Providence manager to hold back the gong for a few minutes.

Presently somebody brought Delaney a telephone message that Red Gilbat was playing ball with some boys in a lot four blocks down the street. When at length a couple of players marched up to the bench with Red in tow Delaney uttered an immense sigh of relief and then, after a close scrutiny of Red's face, he whispered, "Lock the gates!"

Then the gong rang. The Grays trooped in. The Stars ran out, except Gilbat, who ambled like a giraffe. The hum of conversation in the grandstand quickened for a moment with the scraping of chairs, and then grew quiet. The bleachers sent up the rollicking cry of expectancy. The umpire threw out a white ball with his stentorian "Play!" and Blake of the Grays strode to the plate.

Hitting safely, he started the game with a rush. With Dorr up, the Star infield played for a bunt. Like clockwork Dorr dumped the first ball as Blake got his flying start for second base. Morrissey tore in for the ball, got it on the run and snapped it underhand to Healy, beating the runner by an inch. The fast Blake, with a long slide, made third base. The stands stamped. The bleachers howled. White, next man up, batted a high fly to left field. This was a sun field and the hardest to play in the league. Red Gilbat was the only man who ever played it well. He judged the fly, waited under it, took a step back, then forward, and deliberately caught the ball in his gloved hand. A throw-in to catch the runner scoring from third base would have been futile, but it was not like Red Gilbat to fail to try. He tossed the ball to O'Brien. And Blake scored amid applause.

"What do you know about that?" ejaculated Delaney, wiping his moist face. "I never before saw our nutty Redhead pull off a play like that."

Some of the players yelled at Red, "This is a two-handed league, you bat!"

The first five players on the list for the Grays were left-handed batters, and against a right-handed pitcher whose most effective ball for them was a high fast one over the outer corner they would naturally hit toward left field. It was no surprise to see Hanley bat a skyscraper out to left. Red had to run to get under it. He braced himself rather unusually for a fielder. He tried to catch the ball in his bare right hand and muffed it. Hanley got to second on the play while the audience roared. When they got through there was some roaring among the Rochester players. Scott and Captain Healy roared at Red, and Red roared back at them.

"It's all off. Red never did that before," cried Delaney in despair. "He's gone clean bughouse now."

Babcock was the next man up and he likewise hit to left. It was a low, twisting ball—half fly, half liner—and a difficult one to field. Gilbat ran with great bounds, and though he might have got two hands on the ball he did not try, but this time caught it in his right, retiring the side.

The Stars trotted in, Scott and Healy and Kane, all veterans, looking like thunderclouds. Red ambled in the last and he seemed very nonchalant.

"By Gosh, I'd 'a' ketched that one I muffed if I'd had time to change hands," he said with a grin, and he exposed a handful of peanuts. He had refused to drop the peanuts to make the catch with two hands. That explained the mystery. It was funny, yet nobody laughed. There was that run chalked up against the Stars, and this game had to be won.

"Red, I—I want to take the team home in the lead," said Delaney, and it was plain that he suppressed strong feeling. "You didn't play the game, you know."

Red appeared mightily ashamed.

"Del, I'll git that run back," he said.

Then he strode to the plate, swinging his wagon-tongue bat. For all his awkward position in the box he looked what he was—a formidable hitter. He seemed to tower over the pitcher—Red was six feet one—and he scowled and shook his bat at Wehying and called, "Put one over—you wienerwurst!" Wehying was anything but redheaded, and he wasted so many balls on Red that it looked as if he might pass him. He would have passed him, too, if Red had not stepped over on the fourth ball and swung on it. White at second base leaped high for the stinging hit, and failed to reach it. The ball struck and bounded for the fence. When Babcock fielded it in, Red was standing on third base, and the bleachers groaned.

Whereupon Chesty Reddy Clammer proceeded to draw attention to himself, and incidentally delay the game, by assorting the bats as if the audience and the game might gladly wait years to see him make a choice.

"Git in the game!" yelled Delaney.

"Aw, take my bat, Duke of the Abrubsky!" sarcastically said Dump Kane. When the grouchy Kane offered to lend his bat matters were critical in the Star camp.

Other retorts followed, which Reddy Clammer deigned not to notice. At last he got a bat that suited him —and then, importantly, dramatically, with his cap jauntily riding his red locks, he marched to the plate.

Some wag in the bleachers yelled into the silence, "Oh, Maggie, your lover has come!"

Not improbably Clammer was thinking first of his presence before the multitude, secondly of his batting average, and thirdly of the run to be scored. In this instance he waited and feinted at balls and fouled strikes at length to work his base. When he got to first base suddenly he bolted for second, and in the surprise of the unlooked-for play he made it by a spread-eagle slide. It was a circus steal.

Delaney snorted. Then the look of profound disgust vanished in a flash of light. His huge face beamed.

Reddie Ray was striding to the plate.

There was something about Reddie Ray that pleased all the senses. His lithe form seemed instinct with life; any sudden movement was suggestive of stored lightning. His position at the plate was on the left side, and he stood perfectly motionless, with just a hint of tense waiting alertness. Dorr, Blake and Babcock, the outfielders for the Grays, trotted round to the right of their usual position. Delaney smiled derisively, as if he knew how futile it was to tell what field Reddie Ray might hit into. Wehying, the old fox, warily eyed the youngster, and threw him a high curve, close in. It grazed Reddie's shirt, but he never moved a hair. Then Wehying, after the manner of many veteran pitchers when trying out a new and menacing batter, drove a straight fast ball at Reddie's head. Reddie ducked, neither too slow nor too quick, just right to show what an eye he had, how hard it was to pitch to. The next was a strike. And on the next he appeared to step and swing in one action. There was a ringing rap, and the ball shot toward right, curving down, a vicious, headed hit. Mallory, at first base, snatched at it and found only the air. Babcock had only time to take a few sharp steps, and then he plunged down, blocked the hit and fought the twisting ball. Reddie turned first base, flitted on toward second, went headlong in the dust, and shot to the base before White got the throw-in from Babcock. Then, as White wheeled and lined the ball home to catch the scoring Clammer, Reddie Ray leaped up, got his sprinter's start and, like a rocket, was off for third. This time he dove behind the base, sliding in a half circle, and as Hanley caught Strickland's perfect throw and whirled with the ball, Reddie's hand slid to the bag.

Reddie got to his feet amid a rather breathless silence. Even the coachers were quiet. There was a moment of relaxation, then Wehying received the ball from Hanley and faced the batter.

This was Dump Kane. There was a sign of some kind, almost imperceptible, between Kane and Reddie. As Wehying half turned in his swing to pitch, Reddie Ray bounded homeward. It was not so much the boldness of his action as the amazing swiftness of it that held the audience spellbound. Like a thunderbolt Reddie came down the line, almost beating Wehying's pitch to the plate. But Kane's bat intercepted the ball, laying it down, and Reddie scored without sliding. Dorr, by sharp work, just managed to throw Kane out.

Three runs so quick it was hard to tell how they had come. Not in the major league could there have been faster work. And the ball had been fielded perfectly and thrown perfectly.

"There you are," said Delaney, hoarsely. "Can you beat it? If you've been wonderin' how the cripped Stars won so many games just put what you've seen in your pipe and smoke it. Red Gilbat gets on—Reddy Clammer gets on—and then Reddie Ray drives them home or chases them home."

The game went on, and though it did not exactly drag it slowed down considerably. Morrissey and Healy were retired on infield plays. And the sides changed. For the Grays, O'Brien made a scratch hit, went to second on Strickland's sacrifice, stole third, and scored on Mallory's infield out. Wehying missed three strikes. In the Stars' turn the three end players on the batting list were easily disposed of. In the third inning the clever Blake, aided by a base on balls and a hit following, tied the score, and once more struck fire and brimstone from the impatient bleachers. Providence was a town that had to have its team win.

"Git at 'em, Reds!" said Delaney gruffly.

"Batter up!" called Umpire Fuller, sharply.

"Where's Red? Where's the bug? Where's the nut? Delaney, did you lock the gates? Look under the bench!" These and other remarks, not exactly elegant, attested to the mental processes of some of the Stars. Red Gilbat did not appear to be forthcoming. There was an anxious delay. Captain Healy searched for the missing player. Delaney did not say anymore.

Suddenly a door under the grandstand opened and Red Gilbat appeared. He hurried for his bat and then up to the plate. And he never offered to hit one of the balls Wehying shot over. When Fuller had called the third strike Red hurried back to the door and disappeared.

"Somethin' doin'," whispered Delaney.

Lord Chesterfield Clammer paraded to the batter's box and, after gradually surveying the field, as if picking out the exact place he meant to drive the ball, he stepped to the plate. Then a roar from the bleachers surprised him.

"Well, I'll be doggoned!" exclaimed Delaney. "Red stole that sure as shootin'."

Red Gilbat was pushing a brand-new baby carriage toward the batter's box. There was a tittering in the grandstand; another roar from the bleachers. Clammer's face turned as red as his hair. Gilbat shoved the baby carriage upon the plate, spread wide his long arms, made a short presentation speech and an elaborate bow, then backed away.

All eyes were centered on Clammer. If he had taken it right the incident might have passed without undue hilarity. But Clammer became absolutely wild with rage. It was well known that he was unmarried. Equally well was it seen that Gilbat had executed one of his famous tricks. Ball players were inclined to be dignified about the presentation of gifts upon the field, and Clammer, the dude, the swell, the lady's man, the favorite of the baseball gods —in his own estimation—so far lost control of himself that he threw his bat at his retreating tormentor. Red jumped high and the bat skipped along the ground toward the bench. The players sidestepped and leaped and, of course, the bat cracked one of Delaney's big shins. His eyes popped with pain, but he could not stop laughing. One by one the players lay down and rolled over and yelled. The superior Clammer was not overliked by his co-players.

From the grandstand floated the laughter of ladies and gentlemen. And from the bleachers—that throne of the biting, ironic, scornful fans—pealed up a howl of delight. It lasted for a full minute. Then, as quiet ensued, some boy blew a blast of one of those infernal little instruments of pipe and rubber balloon, and over the field wailed out a shrill, high-keyed cry, an excellent imitation of a baby. Whereupon the whole audience roared, and in discomfiture Reddy Clammer went in search of his bat.

To make his chagrin all the worse he ingloriously struck out. And then he strode away under the lea of the grandstand wall toward right field.

Reddie Ray went to bat and, with the infield playing deep and the outfield swung still farther round to the right, he bunted a little teasing ball down the third-base line. Like a flash of light he had crossed first base before Hanley got his hands on the ball. Then Kane hit into second base, forcing Reddie out.

Again the game assumed less spectacular and more ordinary play. Both Scott and Wehying held the batters safely and allowed no runs. But in the fifth inning, with the Stars at bat and two out, Red Gilbat again electrified the field. He sprang up from somewhere and walked to the plate, his long shape enfolded in a full-length linen duster. The color and style of this garment might not have been especially striking, but upon Red it had a weird and wonderful effect. Evidently Red intended to bat while arrayed in his long coat, for he stepped into the box and faced the pitcher. Captain Healy yelled for him to take the duster off. Likewise did the Grays yell.

The bleachers shrieked their disapproval. To say the least, Red Gilbat's crazy assurance was dampening to the ardor of the most blindly confident fans. At length Umpire Fuller waved his hand, enjoining silence and calling time.

"Take it off or I'll fine you."

From his lofty height Gilbat gazed down upon the little umpire, and it was plain what he thought.

"What do I care for money!" replied Red.

"That costs you twenty-five," said Fuller.

"Cigarette change!" yelled Red.

"Costs you fifty."

"Bah! Go to an eye doctor," roared Red.

"Seventy-five," added Fuller, imperturbably.

"Make it a hundred!"

"It's two hundred."

"Rob-b-ber!" bawled Red.

Fuller showed willingness to overlook Red's back talk as well as costume, and he called, "Play!"

There was a mounting sensation of prophetic certainty. Old fox Wehying appeared nervous. He wasted two balls on Red; then he put one over the plate, and then he wasted another. Three balls and one strike! That was a bad place for a pitcher, and with Red Gilbat up it was worse. Wehying swung longer and harder to get all his left behind the throw and let drive. Red lunged and cracked the ball. It went up and up and kept going up and farther out, and as the murmuring audience was slowly transfixed into late realization the ball soared to its height and dropped beyond the left-field fence. A home run!

Red Gilbat gathered up the tails of his duster, after the manner of a neat woman crossing a muddy street, and ambled down to first base and on to second, making prodigious jumps upon the bags, and round third, to come down the homestretch wagging his red head. Then he stood on the plate, and, as if to exact revenge from the audience for the fun they made of him, he threw back his shoulders and bellowed: *"Haw! Haw! Haw!"*

Not a handclap greeted him, but some mindless, exceedingly adventurous fan yelled: "Redhead! Redhead! Redhead!"

That was the one thing calculated to rouse Red Gilbat. He seemed to flare, to bristle, and he paced for the bleachers.

Delaney looked as if he might have a stroke. "Grab him! Soak him with a bat! Somebody grab him!"

But none of the Stars was risking so much, and Gilbat, to the howling derision of the gleeful fans, reached the bleachers. He stretched his long arms up to the fence and prepared to vault over. "Where's the guy who called me redhead?" he yelled.

That was heaping fuel on the fire. From all over the bleachers, from everywhere, came the obnoxious word. Red heaved himself over the fence and piled into the fans. Then followed the roar of many voices, the tramping of many feet, the pressing forward of line after line of shirt-sleeved men and boys. That bleacher stand suddenly assumed the maelstrom appearance of a surging mob round an agitated center. In a moment all the players rushed down the field, and confusion reigned.

"Oh! Oh! Oh!" moaned Delaney.

However, the game had to go on. Delaney, no doubt, felt all was over. Nevertheless, there were games occasionally that seemed an unending series of unprecedented events. This one had begun admirably to break a record. And the Providence fans, like all other fans, had cultivated an appetite as the game proceeded. They were wild to put the other redheads out of the field or at least out for the inning, wild to tie the score, wild to win and wilder than all for more excitement. Clammer hit safely.

But when Reddie Ray lined to the second baseman, Clammer, having taken a lead, was doubled up in the play.

Of course, the sixth inning opened with the Stars playing only eight men. There was another delay. Probably everybody except Delaney, and perhaps Healy, had forgotten the Stars were short a man. Fuller called time. The impatient bleachers barked for action.

Captain White came over to Delaney and courteously offered to lend a player for the remaining innings. Then a pompous individual came out of the door leading from the press boxes—he was a director Delaney disliked.

"Guess you'd better let Fuller call the game," he said brusquely.

"If you want to—as the score stands now in our favor," replied Delaney.

"Not on your life! It'll be ours or else we'll play it out and beat you to death."

He departed in high dudgeon.

"Tell Reddie to swing over a little toward left," was Delaney's order to Healy. Fire gleamed in the manager's eye.

Fuller called play then, with Reddy Clammer and Reddie Ray composing the Star outfield. And the Grays evidently prepared to do great execution through the wide lanes thus opened up. At that stage it would not have been like matured ball players to try to crop hits down into the infield.

White sent a long fly back of Clammer. Reddy had no time to loaf on this hit. It was all he could do to reach it and he made a splendid catch, for which the crowd roundly applauded him. That applause was wine to Reddy Clammer. He began to prance on his toes and sing out to Scott: "Make 'em hit to me, old man! Make 'em hit to me!" Whether Scott desired that or not was scarcely possible to say; at any rate, Hanley pounded a hit through the infield. And Clammer, prancing high in the air like a check-reined horse, ran to intercept the ball. He could have received it in his hands, but that would never have served Reddy Clammer. He timed the hit to a nicety, went down with his old grandstand play and blocked the ball with his anatomy. Delaney swore. And the bleachers, now warm toward the gallant outfielder, lustily cheered him. Babcock hit down the right-field foul line, giving Clammer a long run. Hanley was scoring and Babcock was sprinting for third base when Reddy got the ball. He had a fine arm and he made a hard and accurate throw, catching his man in a close play.

Perhaps even Delaney could not have found any fault with that play. But the aftermath spoiled the thing. Clammer now rode the air; he soared; he was in the clouds; it was his inning and he had utterly forgotten his team mates, except inasmuch as they were performing mere little automatic movements to direct the great machinery in his direction for his sole achievement and glory.

There is fate in baseball as well as in other walks of life. O'Brien was a strapping fellow and he lifted another ball into Clammer's wide territory. The hit was of the high and far-away variety. Clammer started to run with it, not like a grim outfielder, but like one thinking of himself, his style, his opportunity, his inevitable success. Certain it was that in thinking of himself the outfielder forgot his surroundings. He ran across the foul line, head up, hair flying, unheeding the warning cry from Healy. And. reaching up to make his crowning circus play, he smashed face forward into the bleachers fence. Then, limp as a rag. he dropped. The audience sent forth a long groan of sympathy.

"That wasn't one of his stage falls," said Delaney. "I'll bet he's dead . . . Poor Reddy! And I want him to bust his face!"

Clammer was carried off the field into the dressing

room and a physician was summoned out of the audience.

"Cap, what'd it—do to him?" asked Delaney.

"Aw, spoiled his pretty mug, that's all," replied Healy, scornfully. "Mebee he'll listen to me now."

Delaney's change was characteristic of the man. "Well, if it didn't kill him I'm blamed glad he got it . . . Cap, we can trim 'em yet. Reddie Ray'll play the whole outfield. Give Reddie a chance to run! Tell the boy to cut loose. And all of you git in the game. Win or lose, I won't forget it. I've a hunch. Once in a while I can tell what's comin' off. Some queer game this! And we're goin' to win. Gilbat lost the game; Clammer throwed it away again; and now Reddie Ray's due to win it. . . . I'm all in, but I wouldn't miss the finish to save my life."

Delaney's deep presaging sense of baseball events was never put to a greater test. And the seven Stars, with the score tied, exhibited the temper and timber of a championship team in the last ditch. It was so splendid that almost instantly it caught the antagonistic bleachers.

Wherever the tired Scott found renewed strength and speed was a mystery. But he struck out the hard-hitting Providence catcher and that made the third out. The Stars could not score in their half of the inning. Likewise the seventh inning passed without a run for either side; only the infield work of the Stars was something superb. When the eighth inning ended, without a tally for either team, the excitement grew tense. There was Reddie Ray playing outfield alone, and the Grays with all their desperate endeavors had not lifted the ball out of the infield.

But in the ninth, Blake, the first man up, lined low toward right center. The hit was safe and looked good for three bases. No one looking, however, had calculated on Reddie Ray's fleetness. He covered ground and dove for the bounding ball and knocked it down. Blake did not get beyond first base. The crowd cheered the play equally with the prospect of a run. Dorr bunted and beat the throw. White hit one of the high fast balls Scott was serving and sent it close to the left-field foul line. The running Reddie Ray made on that play held White at second base. But two runs had scored with no one out.

Hanley, the fourth left-handed hitter, came up and Scott pitched to him as he had to the others—high fast balls over the inside corner of the plate. Reddie Ray's position was some fifty yards behind deep short, and a little toward center field. He stood sideways, facing two-thirds of that vacant outfield. In spite of Scott's skill, Hanley swung the ball far round into right field, but he hit it high, and almost before he actually hit it the great sprinter was speeding across the green.

The suspense grew almost unbearable as the ball soared in its parabolic flight and the redhaired runner streaked dark across the green. The ball seemed never to be coming down. And when it began to descend and reached a point perhaps fifty feet above the ground there appeared more distance between where it would alight and where Reddie was than anything human could cover. It dropped and dropped, and then dropped into Reddie Ray's outstretched hands. He had made the catch look easy. But the fact that White scored from second base on the play showed what the catch really was.

There was no movement or restlessness of the audience such as usually indicated the beginning of the exodus. Scott struck Babcock out. The game still had fire. The Grays never let up a moment on their coaching. And the hoarse voices of the Stars were grimmer than ever. Reddie Ray was the only one of the seven who kept silent. And he crouched like a tiger.

The teams changed sides with the Grays three runs in the lead. Morrissey, for the Stars, opened with a clean drive to right. Then Healy slashed a ground ball to Hanley and nearly knocked him down. When old Burns, by a hard rap to short, advanced the runners a base and made a desperate, though unsuccessful, effort to reach first the Providence crowd awoke to a strange and inspiring appreciation. They began that most rare feature in baseball audiences—a strong and trenchant call for the visiting team to win.

The play had gone fast and furious. Wehying, sweaty and disheveled, worked violently. All the Grays were on uneasy tiptoes. And the Stars were seven Indians on the warpath. Halloran fouled down the right-field line; then he fouled over the left-field fence. Wehying tried to make him too anxious, but it was in vain. Halloran was implacable. With two strikes and three balls he hit straight down to White, and was out. The ball had been so sharp that neither runner on base had a chance to advance.

Two men out, two on base, Stars wanting three runs to tie, Scott, a weak batter, at the plate! The situation was disheartening. Yet there sat Delaney, shot through and through with some vital compelling force. He saw only victory. And when the very first ball pitched to Scott hit him on the leg, giving him his base, Delaney got to his feet, unsteady and hoarse.

Bases full, Reddie Ray up, three runs to tie!

Delaney looked at Reddie. And Reddie looked at Delaney. The manager's face was pale, intent, with a little smile. The player had eyes of fire, a lean, bulging jaw, and the hands he reached for his bat clutched like talons.

"Reddie, I knew it was waitin' for you," said Delaney, his voice ringing. "Break up the game!"

After all this was only a baseball game, and perhaps from the fans' viewpoint a poor game at that. But the moment when that lithe, redhaired athlete toed the plate was a beautiful one. The long crash from the bleachers, the steady cheer from the grandstand, proved that it was not so much the game that mattered.

Wehying had shot his bolt; he was tired. Yet he made

ready for a final effort. It seemed that passing Reddie Ray on balls would have been a wise play at that juncture. But no pitcher, probably, would have done it with the bases crowded and chances, of course, against the batter.

Clean and swift, Reddie leaped at the first pitched ball. Ping! For a second no one saw the hit. Then it gleamed, a terrific drive, low along the ground, like a bounding bullet, straight at Babcock in right field. It struck his hands and glanced viciously away to roll toward the fence.

Thunder broke loose from the stands. Reddie Ray was turning first base. Beyond first base he got into his wonderful stride. Some runners run with a consistent speed, the best they can make for a given distance. But this trained sprinter gathered speed as he ran. He was no short-stepping runner. His strides were long. They gave an impression of strength combined with fleetness. He had the speed of a racehorse, but the trimness, the raciness, the delicate legs were not characteristic of him. Like the wind he turned second, so powerful that his turn was short. All at once there came a difference in his running. It was no longer beautiful. The grace was gone. It was now fierce, violent. His momentum was running him off his legs. He whirled around third base and came hurtling down the homestretch. His face was convulsed, his eyes were wild. His arms and legs worked in a marvelous muscular velocity. He seemed a demon—a flying streak. He overtook and ran down the laboring Scott, who had almost reached the plate.

The park seemed full of shrill, piercing strife. It swelled, reached a highest pitch, sustained that for a long moment, and then declined.

"My Gawd!" exclaimed Delaney, as he fell back. "Wasn't that a finish? Didn't I tell you to watch them redheads?"

The Rube

I was the most critical time I had yet experienced in my career as a baseball manager. And there was more than the usual reason why I must pull the team out. A chance for a business deal depended upon the goodwill of the stockholders of the Worcester club. On the outskirts of the town was a little cottage that I wanted to buy, and this depended upon the business deal. My whole future happiness depended upon the little girl I hoped to install in that cottage.

Coming to the Worcester Eastern League team, I had found a strong aggregation and an enthusiastic following. I really had a team with pennant possibilities. Providence was a strong rival, but I beat them three straight in the opening series, set a fast pace, and likewise set Worcester baseball mad. The Eastern League clubs were pretty evenly matched; still I continued to hold the lead until misfortune overtook me.

Gregg smashed an umpire and had to be laid off. Mullaney got spiked while sliding and was out of the game. Ashwell sprained his ankle and Hirsch broke a finger. Radbourne, my great pitcher, hurt his arm on a cold day and he could not get up his old speed. Stringer, who had batted .371 and led the league the year before, struck a bad spell and could not hit a barn door handed up to him.

Then came the slump. The team suddenly let down; went to pieces; played ball that would have disgraced an amateur nine. It was a trying time. Here was a great team, strong everywhere. A little hard luck had dug up a slump —and now! Day by day the team dropped in the race. When we reached the second division the newspapers flayed us. Worcester would never stand for a second division team. Baseball admirers, reporters, fans—especially the fans—are fickle. The admirers quit, the reporters grilled us, and the fans, though they stuck to the games with that barnacle-like tenacity peculiar to them, made life miserable for all of us. I saw the pennant slowly fading, and the successful season, and the business deal, and the cottage, and Milly. . . .

But when I thought of her I just could not see failure. Something must be done, but what? I was at the end of my wits. When Jersey City beat us that Saturday, eleven to two, shoving us down to fifth place with only a few percentage points above the Fall River team, I grew desperate, and locking my players in the dressing room I went after them. They had lain down on me and needed a jar. I told them so straight and flat, and being bitter, I did not pick and choose my words.

"And fellows," I concluded, "you've got to brace. A little more of this and we can't pull out. I tell you you're a championship team. We had that pennant cinched. A few cuts and sprains and hard luck—and you all quit! You lay down! I've been patient. I've plugged for you. Never a man have I fined or thrown down. But now I'm at the end of my string. I'm out to fine you now, and I'll release the first man who shows the least yellow. I play no more substitutes. Crippled or not, you guys have got to get in the game."

I waited to catch my breath and expected some such outburst as managers usually get from criticized players. But not a word! Then I addressed some of them personally.

"Gregg, your lay-off ends today. You play Monday. Mullaney, you've drawn your salary for two weeks with that spiked foot. If you can't run on it—well, all right, but I put it up to your good faith. I've played the game and I know it's hard to run on a sore foot. But you can do it. Ashwell, your ankle is lame, I know—now, can you run?"

"Sure I can. I'm not a quitter. I'm ready to go in," replied Ashwell.

"Raddy, how about you?" I said, turning to my star twirler.

"Connelly, I've seen as fast a team in as bad a rut and yet pull out," returned Radbourne. "We're about due for the brace. When it comes—look out! As for me, well, my arm isn't right, but it's acting these warm days in a way that tells me it will be soon. It's been worked too hard. Can't you get another pitcher? I'm not knocking Herne or Cairns. They're good for their turn, but we need a new man to help out. And he must be a crackerjack if we're to get back to the lead."

"Where on earth can I find such a pitcher?" I shouted, almost distracted.

"Well, that's up to you," replied Radbourne.

Up to me it certainly was, and I cudgeled my brains for inspiration. After I had given up in hopelessness it came in the shape of a notice I read in one of the papers. It was a brief mention of an amateur Worcester ball team being shut out in a game with a Rickettsville nine. Rickettsville played Sunday ball, which gave me an opportunity to look them over.

It took some train riding and then a journey by coach to get to Rickettsville. I mingled with the crowd of talking rustics. There was only one little "bleachers" and this was loaded to the danger point with the feminine adherents of the teams. Most of the crowd centered alongside and back of the catcher's box. I edged in and got a position just behind the stone that served as home plate.

Hunting up a player in this way was no new thing to me. I was too wise to make myself known before I had sized up the merits of my man. So, before the players came upon the field I amused myself watching the rustic fans and listening to them. Then a roar announced the appearance of the Rickettsville team and their opponents, who wore the name of Spatsburg on their Canton flannel shirts. The uniforms of these country amateurs would have put a Philadelphia Mummer's parade to the blush, at least for bright colors. But after one amused glance I got down to the stern business of the day, and that was to discover a pitcher, and failing that, baseball talent of any kind.

Never shall I forget my first glimpse of the Ricketts-ville twirler. He was far over six feet tall and as lean as a fence rail. He had a great shock of light hair, a sunburned, sharp-featured face, wide, sloping shoulders, and arms enormously long. He was about as graceful and had about as much of a baseball walk as a crippled cow.

"He's a rube!" I ejaculated, in disgust and disappointment.

But when I had seen him throw one ball to his catcher I grew as keen as a fox on a scent. What speed he had! I got round closer to him and watched him with sharp, eager eyes. He was a giant. To be sure, he was lean, rawboned as a horse, but powerful. What won me at once was his natural, easy swing. He got the ball away with scarcely any effort. I wondered what he could do when he brought the motion of his body into play.

"Bub, what might be the pitcher's name?" I asked of a boy.

"Huh, mister, his name might be Dennis, but it ain't. Huh!" replied this country youngster. Evidently my question had thrown some implication upon this particular player.

"I reckon you be a stranger in these parts," said a pleasant old fellow. "His name's Hurtle—Whitaker Hurtle. Whit for short. He hain't lost a gol-darned game this summer. No sir-ee! Never pitched any before, nuther."

Hurtle! What a remarkably fitting name!

Rickettsville chose the field and the game began. Hurtle swung with his easy motion. The ball shot across like a white bullet. It was a strike, and so was the next, and the one succeeding. He could not throw anything but strikes, and it seemed the Spatsburg players could not make even a foul.

Outside of Hurtle's work the game meant little to me. And I was so fascinated by what I saw in him that I could hardly contain myself. After the first few innings I no longer tried to. I yelled with the Rickettsville rooters. The man was a wonder. A blind baseball manager could have seen that. He had a straight ball, shoulder high, level as a stretched string, and fast. He had a jump ball, which he evidently worked by putting on a little more steam, and it was the speediest thing I ever saw in the way of a shoot. He had a wide-sweeping outcurve, wide as the blade of a mowing scythe. And he had a drop—an unhittable drop. He did not use it often, for it made his catcher dig too hard into the dirt. But whenever he did I glowed all over. Once or twice he used an underhand motion and sent in a ball that fairly swooped up. It could not have been hit with a board. And best of all, dearest to the manager's heart, he had control. Every ball he threw went over the plate. He could not miss it. To him that plate was as big as a house.

What a find! Already I had visions of the long-looked-for brace of my team, and of the pennant, and the little cottage, and the happy light of a pair of blue eyes. What he meant to me, that country pitcher Hurtle! He shut out the Spatsburg team without a run or a hit or even a scratch. Then I went after him. I collared him and his manager, and there, surrounded by the gaping players, I bought him and signed him before any of them knew exactly what I was about. I did not haggle. I asked the manager what he wanted and produced the cash; I asked Hurtle what he wanted, doubled his ridiculously modest demand, paid him in advance, and got his name to the contract. Then I breathed a long, deep breath; the first one for weeks. Something told me that with Hurtle's signature in my pocket I had the Eastern League pennant. Then I invited all concerned down to the Rickettsville hotel.

We made connections at the railroad junction and reached Worcester at midnight in time for a good sleep. I took the silent and backward pitcher to my hotel. In the morning we had breakfast together. I showed him about Worcester and then carried him off to the ball grounds.

I had ordered morning practice, and as morning practice is not conducive to the cheerfulness of ball players, I wanted to reach the dressing room a little late. When we arrived, all the players had dressed and were out on the field. I had some difficulty in fitting Hurtle with a uniform, and when I did get him dressed he resembled a two-legged giraffe decked out in white shirt, gray trousers and maroon stockings.

Spears, my veteran first baseman and captain of the team, was the first to see us.

"Sufferin' umpires!" yelled Spears. "Here, you Micks! Look at this Con's got with him!"

What a yell burst from that sore and disgruntled bunch of ball tossers! My players were a grouchy set in practice anyway, and today they were in their meanest mood.

"Hey, beanpole!"

"Get onto the stilts!"

"Con, where did you find that?"

I cut short their chaffing with a sharp order for bat-ting practice.

"Regular line-up, now no monkey biz," I went on. "Take two cracks and a bunt. Here, Hurtle," I said, draw-ing him toward the pitcher's box, "don't pay any atten-tion to their talk. That's only the fun of ball players. Go in now and practice a little. Lam a few over."

Hurtle's big freckled hands closed nervously over the ball. I thought it best not to say more to him, for he had a rather wild look. I remembered my own stage fright upon my first appearance in fast company. Besides I knew what my amiable players would say to him. I had a secret hope and belief that presently they would yell upon the other side of the fence.

McCall, my speedy little left fielder, led off at bat. He was full of ginger, chipper as a squirrel, sarcastic as only a tried ball player can be.

"Put 'em over, Slats, put 'em over," he called, vi-ciously swinging his ash.

Hurtle stood stiff and awkward in the box and seemed to be rolling something in his mouth. Then he moved his arm. We all saw the ball dart down straight—that is, all of us except McCall, because if he had seen it he might have jumped out of the way. Crack! The ball hit him on the shin.

McCall shrieked. We all groaned. That crack hurt all of us. Any baseball player knows how it hurts to be hit on the shinbone. McCall waved his bat madly.

"Rube! Rube! Rube!" he yelled.

Then and there Hurtle got the name that was to cling to him all his baseball days.

McCall went back to the plate, red in the face, mad as a hornet, and he sidestepped every time Rube pitched a ball. He never even ticked one and retired in disgust, limping and swearing. Ashwell was next. He did not show much alacrity. On Rube's first pitch down went Ashwell flat in the dust. The ball whipped the hair of his head. Rube was wild and I began to get worried. Ashwell hit a couple of measly punks, but when he assayed a bunt the gang yelled derisively at him.

"What's he got?" The old familiar cry of batters when facing a new pitcher!

Stringer went up, bold and formidable. That was what made him the great hitter he was. He loved to bat; he would have faced anybody; he would have faced even a cannon. New curves were a fascination to him. And speed for him, in his own words, was "apple pie." In this instance, surprise was in store for Stringer. Rube shot up the straight one, then the wide curve, then the drop. Stringer missed them all, struck out, fell down ignominiously. It was the first time he had fanned that season and he looked dazed. We had to haul him away.

I called off the practice, somewhat worried about Rube's showing, and undecided whether or not to try him in the game that day. So I went to Radbourne, who had quietly watched Rube while on the field. Raddy was an old pitcher and had seen the rise of a hundred stars. I told him about the game at Rickettsville and what I thought of Rube, and frankly asked his opinion.

"Con, you've made the find of your life," said Raddy, quietly and deliberately.

This from Radbourne was not only comforting; it was relief, hope, assurance. I avoided Spears, for it would hardly be possible for him to regard the Rube favorably, and I kept under cover until time to show up at the grounds.

Buffalo was on the ticket for that afternoon, and the Bisons were leading the race and playing in topnotch form. I went into the dressing room while the players were changing suits, because there was a little unpleasantness that I wanted to spring on them before we got on the field.

"Boys," I said, curtly, "Hurtle works today. Cut loose, now, and back him up."

I had to grab a bat and pound on the wall to stop the uproar.

"Did you mutts hear what I said? Well, it goes. Not a word, now. I'm handling this team. We're in bad, I know, but it's my judgment to pitch Hurtle, rube or no rube, and it's up to you to back us. That's the baseball of it."

Grumbling and muttering, they passed out of the dressing room. I knew ball players. If Hurtle should happen to show good form they would turn in a flash. Rube tagged reluctantly in their rear. He looked like a man in a trance. I wanted to speak encouragingly to him, but Raddy told me to keep quiet.

It was inspiring to see my team practice that afternoon. There had come a subtle change. I foresaw one of those baseball climaxes that can be felt and seen, but not explained. Whether it was a hint of the hoped-for brace, or only another flash of form before the final letdown, I had no means to tell. But I was on edge.

Carter, the umpire, called out the batteries, and I sent my team into the field. When that long, lanky, awkward rustic started for the pitcher's box, I thought the bleachers would make him drop in his tracks. The fans were sore on anyone those days, and a new pitcher was bound to hear from them.

"Where! Oh, where! Oh, where!"

"Connelly's found another dead one"

"Scarecrow!"

"Look at his pants!"

"Pad his legs!"

Then the inning began, and things happened. Rube had marvelous speed, but he could not find the plate. He threw the ball the second he got it; he hit men, walked men, and fell all over himself trying to field bunts. The crowd stormed and railed and hissed. The Bisons pranced round the bases and yelled like Indians. Finally they retired with eight runs.

Eight runs! Enough to win two games! I could not have told how it happened. I was sick and all but crushed. Still I had a blind, dogged faith in the big rustic. I believed he had not got started right. It was a trying situation. I called Spears and Raddy to my side and talked fast.

"It's all off now. Let the dinged rube take his medicine," growled Spears.

"Don't take him out," said Raddy. "He's not shown at all what's in him. The blamed hayseed is up in the air. He's crazy. He doesn't know what he's doing. I tell you, Con, he may be scared to death, but he's dead in earnest."

Suddenly I recalled the advice of the pleasant old fellow at Rickettsville.

"Spears, you're the captain," I said, sharply. "Go after the rube. Wake him up. Tell him he can't pitch. Call him 'Pogie!' That's a name that stirs him up."

"Well, I'll be dinged! He looks it," replied Spears. "Here, Rube, get off the bench. Come here."

Rube lurched toward us. He seemed to be walking in his sleep. His breast was laboring and he was dripping with sweat.

"Whoever told you that you could pitch?" asked Spears genially. He was master at baseball ridicule. I had never yet seen the youngster who could stand his badinage. He said a few things, then wound up with: "Come now, you cross between a hayrack and a wagon tongue, get sore and do something. Pitch if you can. Show us! Do you hear, you tow-headed Pogie!"

Rube jumped as if he had been struck. His face flamed red and his little eyes turned black. He shoved his big fist under Captain Spears' nose.

"Mister, I'll lick you fer thet—after the game! And I'll show you doggoned well how I can pitch."

"Good!" exclaimed Raddy; and I echoed his word. Then I went to the bench and turned my attention to the game. Someone told me that McCall had made a couple of fouls, and after waiting for two strikes and three balls had struck out. Ashwell had beat out a bunt in his old swift style, and Stringer was walking up to the plate on the moment. It was interesting, even in a losing game, to see Stringer go to bat. We all watched him, as we had been watching him for weeks, expecting him to break his slump with one of the drives that had made him famous. Stringer stood to the left side of the plate, and I could see the bulge of his closely locked jaw. He swung on the first pitched ball. With the solid rap we all rose to watch that hit. The ball lined first, then soared and did not begin to drop till it was far beyond the right-field fence. For an instant we were all still, so were the bleachers. Stringer had broken his slump with the longest drive ever made on the grounds. The crowd cheered as he trotted around the bases behind Ashwell. Two runs.

"Con, how'd you like that drive?" he asked me, with a bright gleam in his eyes.

"Oh! A beaut!" I replied, incoherently. The players on the bench were all as glad as I was. Henley flew out to left. Mullaney smashed a two-bagger to right. Then Gregg hit safely, but Mullaney, in trying to score on the play, was out at the plate.

"Four hits! I tell you fellows, something's coming off," said Raddy. "Now, if only Rube—"

What a difference there was in that long rustic! He stalked into the box, unmindful of the hooting crowd and grimly faced Schultz, the first batter up for the Bisons. This time Rube was deliberate. And where he had not swung before he now got his body and arm into full motion. The ball came in like a glint of light. Schultz looked surprised. The umpire called "Strike!"

"Wow!" yelled the Buffalo coacher. Rube sped up the sidewheeler and Schultz reached wide to meet it and failed. The third was the lightning drop, straight over the plate. The batter poked weakly at it. Then Carl struck out and Manning following, did likewise. Three of the best hitters in the Eastern retired on nine strikes! That was no fluke. I knew what it meant, and I sat there hugging myself with the hum of something joyous in my ears.

Gregg had a glow on his sweaty face. "Oh, but say, boys, take a tip from me! The Rube's a world beater! Raddy knew it; he sized up that swing, and now I know it. Get wise, you its!"

When old Spears pasted a single through shortstop, the Buffalo manager took Clary out of the box and put in Vane, their best pitcher. Bogart advanced the runner to second, but was thrown out on the play. Then Rube came up. He swung a huge bat and loomed over the Bison's twirler. Rube had the look of a hitter. He seemed to be holding himself back from walking right into the ball. And he hit one high and far away. The fast Carl could not get under it, though he made a valiant effort. Spears scored and Rube's long strides carried him to third. The cold crowd in the stands came to life; even the sore bleachers opened up. McCall dumped a slow teaser down the line, a hit that would easily have scored Rube, but he ran a little way, then stopped, tried to get back, and was easily touched out. Ashwell's hard chance gave the Bison's shortstop an error, and Stringer came up with two men on bases. Stringer hit a foul over the right-field fence and the crowd howled. Then he hit a hard long drive straight into the centerfielder's hands.

"Con, I don't know what to think, but ding me if we ain't hittin' the ball," said Spears. Then to his players: "A little more of that and we're back in our old shape. All in a minute—at 'em now! Rube, you dinged old Pogie, pitch!"

Rube toed the rubber, wrapped his long, brown fingers round the ball, stepped out as he swung and—zing! That inning he unloosed a few more kinks in his arm and he tried some new balls upon the Bisons. But whatever he used and wherever he put them the result was the same—they cut the plate and the Bisons were powerless.

That inning marked the change in my team. They had come back. The hoodoo had vanished. The championship Worcester team was itself again.

The Bisons were fighting, too, but Rube had them helpless. When they did hit a ball one of my infielders snapped it up. No chances went to the outfield. I sat there listening to my men, and reveled in a moment that I had long prayed for.

"Now you're pitching some, Rube. Another strike! Get him a board!" called Ashwell.

"Ding 'em, Rube, ding 'em!" came from Captain Spears.

"Speed? Oh—no!" yelled Bogart at third base.

"It's all off, Rube! It's all off—all off!"

So, with the wonderful pitching of an angry rube, the Worcester team came into its own again. I sat through it all without another word; without giving a signal. In a way I realized the awakening of the bleachers, and heard the pound of feet and the crash, but it was the spirit of my team that thrilled me. Next to that the work of my new find absorbed me. I gloated over his easy, deceiving swing. I rose out of my seat when he threw that straight fast ball, swift as a bullet, true as a plumb line. And when those hard-hitting, sure-bunting Bisons chopped in vain at the wonderful drop, I choked back a wild yell. For Rube meant the world to me that day.

In the eighth the score was 8 to 6. The Bisons had one scratch hit to their credit, but not a runner had got beyond first base. Again Rube held them safely, one man striking out, another fouling out, and the third going out on a little fly.

Crash! Crash! Crash! Crash! The bleachers were making up for many games in which they could not express their riotous feelings.

"It's a cinch we'll win!" yelled a fan with a voice. Rube was the first man up in our half of the ninth and his big bat lammed the first ball safe over second base. The crowd, hungry for victory, got to their feet and stayed upon their feet, calling, cheering for runs. It was the moment for me to get in the game, and I leaped up, strung like a wire, and white hot with inspiration. I sent Spears to the coaching box with orders to make Rube run on the first ball. I gripped McCall with hands that made him wince.

Then I dropped back on the bench spent and panting. It was only a game, yet it meant so much! Little McCall was dark as a thundercloud, and his fiery eyes snapped. He was the fastest man in the league, and could have bunted an arrow from a bow. The foxy Bison third baseman edged in. Mac feinted to bunt toward him then turned his bat inward and dumped a teasing curving ball down the first base line. Rube ran as if in seven-league boots. Mac's short legs twinkled; he went like the wind; he leaped into first base with his long slide, and beat the throw.

The stands and bleachers seemed to be tumbling down. For a moment the air was full of deafening sound. Then came the pause, the dying away of clatter and roar, the close waiting, suspended quiet. Spears' clear voice, as he coached Rube, in its keen note seemed inevitable of another run.

Ashwell took his stand. He was another left-hand hitter, and against a right-hand pitcher, in such circumstances as these, the most dangerous of men. Vane knew it. Ellis, the Bison captain knew it, as showed plainly in his signal to catch Rube at second. But Spears' warning held or frightened Rube on the bag.

Vane wasted a ball, then another. Ashwell could not be coaxed. Wearily Vane swung; the shortstop raced out to get in line for a possible hit through the wide space to his right, and the second baseman got on his toes as both base runners started.

Crack! The old story of the hit and run game! Ashwell's hit crossed sharply where a moment before the shortstop had been standing. With gigantic strides Rube rounded the corner and scored. McCall flitted through second, and diving into third with a cloud of dust, got the umpire's decision. When Stringer hurried up with Mac on third and Ash on first the whole field seemed racked in a deafening storm. Again it subsided quickly. The hopes of the Worcester fans had been crushed too often of late for them to be fearless.

But I had no fear. I only wanted the suspense ended. I was like a man clamped in a vise. Stringer stood motionless. Mac bent low with the sprinters' stoop; Ash watched the pitcher's arm and slowly edged off first. Stringer waited for one strike and two balls, then he hit the next. It hugged the first base line, bounced fiercely past the bag and skipped over the grass to bump hard into the fence. McCall romped home, and lame Ashwell beat any run he ever made to the plate. Rolling, swelling, crashing roar of frenzied feet could not down the high piercing sustained yell of the fans. It was great. Three weeks of submerged bottled baseball joy exploded in one mad outburst! The fans, too, had come into their own again.

We scored no more. But the Bisons were beaten. Their spirit was broken. This did not make the Rube let up in their last half inning. Grim and pale he faced them. At every long step and swing he tossed his shock of light hair. At the end he was even stronger than at the beginning. He still had the glancing, floating airy quality that baseball players call speed. And he struck out the last three batters.

In the tumult that burst over my ears I sat staring at the dots on my score card. Fourteen strike outs! One scratch hit! No base on balls since the first inning! That told the story which deadened senses doubted. There was a roar in my ears. Someone was pounding me. As I struggled to get into the dressing room the crowd mobbed me. But I did not hear what they yelled. I had a kind of misty veil before my eyes, in which I saw that lanky Rube magnified into a glorious figure. I saw the pennant waving, and the gleam of a white cottage through the trees, and a trim figure waiting at the gate. Then I rolled into the dressing room.

Somehow it seemed strange to me. Most of the players were stretched out in peculiar convulsions. Old Spears sat with drooping head. Then a wild flaming-eyed giant swooped upon me. With a voice of thunder he announced:

"I'm a-goin' to lick you, too!"

After that we never called him any name except Rube.

The Rube's Waterloo

I T was about the sixth inning that I suspected the Rube
of weakening. For that matter he had not pitched
anything resembling his usual brand of baseball. But the
Rube had developed into such a wonder in the box that it
took time for his letdown to dawn upon me. Also it took a
tip from Raddy, who sat with me on the bench.

"Con, the Rube isn't himself today," said Radbourne.
"His mind's not on the game. He seems hurried and flustered, too. If he doesn't explode presently, I'm a dub at
callin' the turn."

Raddy was the best judge of a pitcher's condition,
physical or mental, in the Eastern League. It was a Saturday and we were on the road and finishing up a series
with the Rochesters. Each team had won and lost a game,
and, as I was climbing close to the leaders in the pennant
race, I wanted the third and deciding game of that Rochester series. The usual big Saturday crowd was in attendance, noisy, demonstrative, and exacting.

In this sixth inning the first man up for Rochester had
flied to McCall. Then had come the two plays significant
of Rube's weakening. He had hit one batter and walked
another. This was sufficient, considering the score was

three to one in our favor, to bring the audience to its feet with a howling, stamping demand for runs.

"Spears is wise all right," said Raddy.

I watched the foxy old captain walk over to the Rube and talk to him while he rested, a reassuring hand on the pitcher's shoulder. The crowd yelled its disapproval and Umpire Bates called out sharply:

"Spears, get back to the bag!"

"Now, Mister Umpire, ain't I hurrin' all I can?" queried Spears as he leisurely ambled back to first.

The Rube tossed a long, damp welt of hair back from his big brow and nervously toed the rubber. I noted that he seemed to forget the runners on bases and delivered the ball without glancing at either bag. Of course this resulted in a double steal. The ball went wild—almost a wild pitch.

"Steady up, old man," called Gregg between the yells of the bleachers. He held his mitt square over the plate for the Rube to pitch to. Again the long twirler took his swing, and again the ball went wild. Clancy had the Rube in the hole now and the situation began to grow serious. The Rube did not take half his usual deliberation, and of the next two pitches one of them was a ball and the other a strike by grace of the umpire's generosity. Clancy rapped the next one, an absurdly slow pitch for the Rube to use, and both runners scored to the shrill tune of the happy bleachers.

I saw Spears shake his head and look toward the bench. It was plain what that meant.

"Raddy, I ought to take the Rube out," I said, "but whom can I put in? You worked yesterday—Cairns' arm is sore. It's got to be nursed. And Henderson, that ladies' man I just signed, is not in uniform."

"I'll go in," replied Raddy, instantly.

"Not on your life." I had as hard a time keeping Radbourne from overworking as I had in getting enough work out of some other players. "I guess I'll let the Rube take his medicine. I hate to lose this game, but if we have to, we can stand it. I'm curious, anyway, to see what's the matter with the Rube. Maybe he'll settle down presently."

I made no sign that I had noticed Spears' appeal to the bench. And my aggressive players, no doubt seeing the situation as I saw it, sang out their various calls of cheer to the Rube and of defiance to their antagonists. Clancy stole off first base so far that the Rube, catching somebody's warning too late, made a balk and the umpire sent the runner on to second. The Rube now plainly showed painful evidences of being rattled.

He could not locate the plate without slowing up and when he did that a Rochester player walloped the ball. Pretty soon he pitched as if he did not care, and but for the fast fielding of the team behind him the Rochesters would have scored more than the eight runs it got. When the Rube came in to the bench I asked him if he was sick and at first he said he was and then that he was not. So I let him pitch the remaining innings, as the game was lost anyhow, and we walked off the field a badly beaten team.

That night we had to hurry from the hotel to catch a train for Worcester and we had dinner in the dining car. Several of my players' wives had come over from Worcester to meet us, and were in the dining car when I entered. I observed a pretty girl sitting at one of the tables with my new pitcher, Henderson.

"Say, Mac," I said to McCall, who was with me, "is Henderson married?"

"Naw, but he looks like he wanted to be. He was in the grandstand today with that girl."

"Who is she? Oh! a little peach!"

A second glance at Henderson's companion brought this compliment from me involuntarily.

"Con, you'll get it as bad as the rest of this mushy bunch of ball players. We're all stuck on that kid. But since Henderson came she's been a frost to all of us. An' it's put the Rube in the dumps.''

"Who's the girl?''

"That's Nan Brown. She lives in Worcester an' is the craziest girl fan I ever seen. Flirt! Well, she's got them all beat. Somebody introduced the Rube to her. He has been mooney ever since.''

That was enough to whet my curiosity, and I favored Miss Brown with more than one glance during dinner. When we returned to the parlor car I took advantage of the opportunity and remarked to Henderson that he might introduce his manager. He complied, but not with amiable grace.

So I chatted with Nan Brown, and studied her. She was a pretty, laughing, coquettish little minx and quite baseball mad. I had met many girl fans, but none so enthusiastic as Nan. But she was wholesome and sincere, and I liked her.

Before turning in I sat down beside the Rube. He was very quiet and his face did not encourage company. But that did not stop me.

"Hello, Whit; have a smoke before you go to bed?'' I asked cheerfully.

He scarcely heard me and made no move to take the proffered cigar. All at once it struck me that the rustic simplicity which had characterized him had vanished.

"Whit, old fellow, what was wrong today?'' I asked, quietly, with my hand on his arm.

"Mr. Connelly, I want my release. I want to go back to Rickettsville,'' he replied hurriedly.

For the space of a few seconds I did some tall thinking. The situation suddenly became grave. I saw the pennant for the Worcesters fading, dimming.

"You want to go home?'' I began slowly. "Why, Whit, I can't keep you. I wouldn't try if you didn't want to stay. But I'll tell you confidentially, if you leave me at this stage I'm ruined."

"How's that?" he inquired, keenly looking at me.

"Well, I can't win the pennant without you. If I do win it there's a big bonus for me. I can buy the house I want and get married this fall if I capture the flag. You've met Milly. You can imagine what your pitching means to me this year. That's all."

He averted his face and looked out of the window. His big jaw quivered.

"If it's that—why, I'll stay, I reckon," he said huskily.

That moment bound Whit Hurtle and Frank Connelly into a far closer relation than the one between player and manager. I sat silent for a while, listening to the drowsy talk of the other players and the rush and roar of the train as it sped on into the night.

"Thank you, old chap," I replied. "It wouldn't have been like you to throw me down at this stage. Whit, you're in trouble?"

"Yes."

"Can I help you—in anyway?"

"I reckon not."

"Don't be too sure of that. I'm a pretty wise guy, if I do say it myself. I might be able to do as much for you as you're going to do for me."

The sight of his face convinced me that I had taken a wrong tack. It also showed me how deep Whit's trouble really was. I bade him good night and went to my berth, where sleep did not soon visit me. A saucy, sparkling-eyed woman barred Whit Hurtle's baseball career at its threshold.

Women are just as fatal to ball players as to men in any other walk of life. I had seen a strong athlete grow palsied just at a scornful slight. It's a great world, and the women run it. So I lay awake racking my brains to outwit a pretty disorganizer; and I plotted for her sake. Married, she would be out of mischief. For Whit's sake, for Milly's sake, for mine, all of which collectively meant for the sake of the pennant, this would be the solution of the problem.

I decided to take Milly into my confidence, and finally on the strength of that I got to sleep. In the morning I went to my hotel, had breakfast, attended to my mail, and then boarded a car to go out to Milly's house. She was waiting for me on the porch, dressed as I liked to see her, in blue and white, and she wore violets that matched the color of her eyes.

"Hello, Connie. I haven't seen a morning paper, but I know from your face that you lost the Rochester series," said Milly, with a gay laugh.

"I guess yes. The Rube blew up, and if we don't play a pretty smooth game, young lady, he'll never come down."

Then I told her.

"Why, Connie, I knew long ago. Haven't you seen the change in him before this?"

"What change?" I asked blankly.

"You are a man. Well, he was a gawky, slouchy, shy farmer boy when he came to us. Of course the city life and popularity began to influence him. Then he met Nan. She made the Rube a worshipper. I first noticed a change in his clothes. He blossomed out in a new suit, white negligee, neat tie, and a stylish straw hat. Then it was evident he was making heroic struggles to overcome his awkwardness. It was plain he was studying and copying the other boys. He's wonderfully improved, but still shy. He'll always be shy. Connie, Whit's a fine fellow, too good for Nan Brown."

"But, Milly," I interrupted, "the Rube's hard hit. Why is he too good for her?"

"Nan is a natural-born flirt," Milly replied. "She can't help it. I'm afraid Whit has a slim chance. Nan may not see deep enough to learn his fine qualities. I fancy Nan tired quickly of him, though the one time I saw them together she appeared to like him very well. This new pitcher of yours, Henderson, is a handsome fellow and smooth. Whit is losing to him. Nan likes flash, flattery, excitement."

"McCall told me the Rube had been down in the mouth ever since Henderson joined the team. Milly, I don't like Henderson a whole lot. He's not in the Rube's class as a pitcher. What am I going to do? Lose the pennant and a big slice of purse money just for a pretty little flirt?"

"Oh, Connie, it's not so bad as that. Whit will come around all right."

"He won't unless we can pull some wires. I've got to help him win Nan Brown. What do you think of that for a manager's job? I guess maybe winning pennants doesn't call for diplomatic genius and cunning! But I'll hand them a few tricks before I lose. My first move will be to give Henderson his release.

I left Milly, as always, once more able to make light of discouragements and difficulties.

Monday I gave Henderson his unconditional release. He celebrated the occasion by verifying certain rumors I had heard from other managers. He got drunk. But he did not leave town, and I heard that he was negotiating with Providence for a place on that team.

Radbourne pitched one of his gilt-edged games that afternoon against Hartford and we won. And Milly sat in the grandstand, having contrived by cleverness to get a seat next to Nan Brown. Milly and I were playing a vastly deeper game than baseball—a game with hearts. But we were playing it with honest motive, for the good of all concerned, we believed, and on the square. I sneaked a look now and then up into the grandstand. Milly and Nan appeared to be getting on famously. It was certain that Nan was flushed and excited, no doubt consciously proud of being seen with my affianced. After the game I chanced to meet them on their way out. Milly winked at me, which was her sign that all was working beautifully.

I hunted up the Rube and bundled him off to the hotel to take dinner with me. At first he was glum, but after a while he brightened up somewhat to my persistent cheer and friendliness. Then we went out on the hotel balcony to smoke, and there I made my play.

"Whit, I'm pulling a stroke for you. Now listen and don't be offended. I know what's put you off your feed, because I was the same way when Milly had me guessing. You've lost your head over Nan Brown. That's not so terrible, though I daresay you think it's a catastrophe. Because you've quit. You've shown a yellow streak. You've lain down.

"My boy, that isn't the way to win a girl. You've got to scrap. Milly told me yesterday how she had watched your love affairs with Nan, and how she thought you had given up just when things might have come your way. Nan is a little flirt, but she's all right. What's more, she was getting fond of you. Nan is meanest to the man she likes best. The way to handle her, Whit, is to master her. Play high and mighty. Get tragical. Then grab her up in your arms. I tell you, Whit, it'll all come your way if you only keep your nerve. I'm your friend and so is Milly. We're going out to her house presently—and Nan will be there."

The Rube drew a long, deep breath and held out his hand. I sensed another stage in the evolution of Whit Hurtle.

"I reckon I've taken baseball coachin'," he said presently, "an' I don't see why I can't take some other kind. I'm only a rube, an' things come hard for me, but I'm a-learnin'."

It was about dark when we arrived at the house.

"Hello, Connie. You're late. Good evening, Mr. Hurtle. Come right in. You've met Miss Nan Brown? Oh, of course; how stupid of me!"

It was a trying moment for Milly and me. A little pallor showed under the Rube's tan, but he was more composed than I had expected. Nan got up from the piano. She was all in white and deliciously pretty. She gave a quick, glad start of surprise. What a relief that was to my troubled mind! Everything had depended upon a real honest liking for Whit, and she had it.

More than once I had been proud of Milly's cleverness, but this night as hostess and an accomplice she won my everlasting admiration. She contrived to give the impression that Whit was a frequent visitor at her home and very welcome. She brought out his best points, and in her skillful hands he lost embarrassment and awkwardness. Before the evening was over Nan regarded Whit with different eyes, and she never dreamed that everything had not come about naturally. Then Milly somehow got me out on the porch, leaving Nan and Whit together.

"Milly, you're a marvel, the best and sweetest ever," I whispered. "We're going to win. It's a cinch."

"Well, Connie, not that—exactly," she whispered back demurely. "But it looks hopeful."

I could not help hearing what was said in the parlor.

"Now I can roast you," Nan was saying, archly. She had switched back to her favorite baseball vernacular. "You pitched a swell game last Saturday in Rochester, didn't you? Not! You had no steam, no control, and you couldn't have curved a saucer."

"Nan, what could you expect?" was the cool reply. "You sat up in the stand with your handsome friend. I reckon I couldn't pitch. I just gave the game away."

"Whit!—Whit!—"

Then I whispered to Milly that it might be discreet for us to move a little way from the vicinity.

It was on the second day afterward that I got a

chance to talk to Nan. She reached the grounds early, before Milly arrived, and I found her in the grandstand. The Rube was down on the card to pitch and when he started to warm up Nan said confidently that he would shut out Hartford that afternoon.

"I'm sorry, Nan, but you're way off. We'd do well to win at all, let alone get a shutout."

"You're a fine manager!" she retorted, hotly. "Why won't we win?"

"Well, the Rube's not in good form. The Rube—"

"Stop calling him that horrid name."

"Whit's not in shape. He's not right. He's ill or something is wrong. I'm worried sick about him."

"Why—Mr. Connelly!" exclaimed Nan. She turned quickly toward me.

I crowded on full canvas of gloom to my already long face.

"I'm serious, Nan. The lad's off, somehow. He's in magnificent physical trim, but he can't keep his mind on the game. He has lost his head. I've talked with him, reasoned with him, all to no good. He only goes down deeper in the dumps. Something is terribly wrong with him, and if he doesn't brace, I'll have to release—"

Miss Nan Brown suddenly lost a little of her rich bloom. "Oh! you wouldn't—you couldn't release him!"

"I'll have to if he doesn't brace. It means a lot to me, Nan, for of course I can't win the pennant this year without Whit being in shape. But I believe I wouldn't mind the loss of that any more than to see him fall down. The boy is a magnificent pitcher. If he can only be brought around he'll go to the big league next year and develop into one of the greatest pitchers the game has ever produced. But somehow or other he has lost heart. He's quit. And I've done my best for him. He's beyond me now. What a shame it is! For he's the making of such a splendid man outside of baseball. Milly thinks the world of him.

Well, well; there are disappointments—we can't help them. There goes the gong. I must leave you. Nan, I'll bet you a box of candy Whit loses today. Is it a go?"

"It is," replied Nan, with fire in her eyes. "You go to Whit Hurtle and tell him I said if he wins today's game I'll kiss him!"

I nearly broke my neck over benches and bats getting to Whit with that message. He gulped once.

Then he tightened his belt and shut out Hartford with two scratch singles. It was a great exhibition of pitching. I had no means to tell whether or not the Rube got his reward that night, but I was so happy that I hugged Milly within an inch of her life.

But it turned out that I had been a little premature in my elation. In two days the Rube went down into the depths again, this time clear to China, and Nan was sitting in the grandstand with Henderson. The Rube lost his next game, pitching like a schoolboy scared out of his wits. Henderson followed Nan like a shadow, so that I had no chance to talk to her. The Rube lost his next game and then another. We were pushed out of second place.

If we kept up that losing streak a little longer, our hopes for the pennant were gone. I had begun to despair of the Rube. For some occult reason he scarcely spoke to me. Nan flirted worse than ever. It seemed to me she flaunted her conquest of Henderson in poor Whit's face.

The Providence ball team came to town and promptly signed Henderson and announced him for Saturday's game. Cairns won the first of the series and Radbourne lost the second. It was Rube's turn to pitch the Saturday game and I resolved to make one more effort to put the lovesick swain in something like his old fettle. So I called upon Nan.

She was surprised to see me, but received me graciously. I fancied her face was not quite so glowing as usual. I came bluntly out with my mission. She tried to freeze me but I would not freeze. I was out to win or lose and not to be lightly laughed aside or coldly denied. I played to make her angry, knowing the real truth of her feelings would show under stress.

For once in my life I became a knocker and said some unpleasant things—albeit they were true—about Henderson. She championed Henderson royally, and when, as a last card, I compared Whit's fine record with Henderson's, not only as a ball player, but as a man, particularly in his reverence for women, she flashed at me:

"What do you know about it? Mr. Henderson asked me to marry him. Can a man do more to show his respect? Your friend never so much as hinted such honorable intentions. What's more—he insulted me!" The blaze in Nan's black eyes softened with a film of tears. She looked hurt. Her pride had encountered a fall.

"Oh, no, Nan, Whit couldn't insult a lady," I protested.

"Couldn't he? That's all you know about him. You know I—I promised to kiss him if he beat Hartford that day. So when he came I—I did. Then the big savage began to rave and he grabbed me up in his arms. He smothered me; almost crushed the life out of me. He frightened me terribly. When I got away from him—the monster stood there and coolly said I belonged to him. I ran out of the room and wouldn't see him anymore. At first I might have forgiven him if he had apologized—said he was sorry, but never a word. Now I never will forgive him."

I had to make a strenuous effort to conceal my agitation. The Rube had most carefully taken my fool advice in the matter of wooing a woman.

When I had got a hold upon myself, I turned to Nan white-hot with eloquence. Now I was talking not wholly for myself or the pennant, but for this boy and girl who were at odds in that strangest game of life—love.

What I said I never knew, but Nan lost her resentment, and then her scorn and indifference. Slowly she thawed and warmed to my reason, praise, whatever it was, and when I stopped she was again the radiant bewildering Nan of old.

"Take another message to Whit for me," she said, audaciously. "Tell him I adore ball players, especially pitchers. Tell him I'm going to the game today to choose the best one. If he loses the game—"

She left the sentence unfinished. In my state of mind I doubted not in the least that she meant to marry the pitcher who won the game, and so I told the Rube. He made one wild upheaval of his arms and shoulders, like an erupting volcano, which proved to me that he believed it, too.

When I got to the bench that afternoon I was tired. There was a big crowd to see the game; the weather was perfect; Milly sat up in the box and waved her score card at me; Raddy and Spears declared we had the game; the Rube stalked to and fro like an implacable Indian chief— but I was not happy in mind. Calamity breathed in the very air.

The game began. McCall beat out a bunt; Ashwell sacrificed and Stringer laced one of his beautiful triples against the fence. Then he scored on a high fly. Two runs! Worcester trotted out into the field. The Rube was white with determination; he had the speed of a bullet and perfect control of his jump ball and drop. But Providence hit and had the luck. Ashwell fumbled, Gregg threw wild. Providence tied the score.

The game progressed, growing more and more of a nightmare to me. It was not Worcester's day. The umpire could not see straight; the boys grumbled and fought among themselves; Spears roasted the umpire and was sent to the bench; Bogart tripped, hurting his sore ankle, and had to be taken out. Henderson's slow, easy ball baffled my players, and when he used speed they lined it straight at a Providence fielder.

In the sixth, after a desperate rally, we crowded the bases with only one out. Then Mullaney's hard rap to left, seemingly good for three bases, was pulled down by Stone with one hand. It was a wonderful catch and he doubled up a runner at second. Again in the seventh we had a chance to score, only to fail on another double play, this time by the infield.

When the Providence players were at bat their luck not only held good but trebled and quadrupled. The little Texas-league hits dropped safely just out of reach of the infielders. My boys had an off day in fielding. What horror that of all days in a season this should be the one for them to make errors!

But they were game, and the Rube was the gamest of all. He did not seem to know what hard luck was, or discouragement, or poor support. He kept everlastingly hammering the ball at those lucky Providence hitters. What speed he had! The ball streaked in, and somebody would shut his eyes and make a safety. But the Rube pitched, on, tireless, irresistibly, hopeful, not forgetting to call a word of cheer to his fielders.

It was one of those strange games that could not be bettered by any labor or daring or skill. I saw it was lost from the second inning, yet so deeply was I concerned, so tantalizingly did the plays reel themselves off, that I groveled there on the bench unable to abide by my baseball sense.

The ninth inning proved beyond a shadow of doubt how baseball fate, in common with other fates, loved to balance the chances, to lift up one, then the other, to lend a deceitful hope only to dash it away.

Providence had almost three times enough to win. The team let up in that inning or grew overconfident or careless, and before we knew what had happened some scratch hits, and bases on balls, and errors, gave us three runs and left two runners on bases. The disgusted bleachers came out of their gloom and began to whistle and thump. The Rube hit safely, sending another run over the plate. McCall worked his old trick, beating out a slow bunt.

Bases full, three runs to tie! With Ashwell up and one out, the noise in the bleachers mounted to a high-pitched, shrill, continuous sound. I got up and yelled with all my might and could not hear my voice. Ashwell was a dangerous man in a pinch. The game was not lost yet. A hit, anything to get Ash to first—and then Stringer!

Ash laughed at Henderson, taunted him, shook his bat at him and dared him to put one over. Henderson did not stand under fire. The ball he pitched had no steam. Ash cracked it—square on the line into the shortstop's hands. The bleachers ceased yelling.

Then Stringer strode grimly to the plate. It was a hundred to one, in that instance, that he would lose the ball. The bleachers let out one deafening roar, then hushed. I would rather have had Stringer at the bat than any other player in the world, and I thought of the Rube and Nan and Milly—and hope would not die.

Stringer swung mightily on the first pitch and struck the ball with a sharp, solid bing! It shot toward center, low, level, exceedingly swift, and like a dark streak went straight into the fielder's hands. A rod to right or left would have made it a home run. The crowd strangled a victorious yell. I came out of my trance, for the game was over and lost. It was the Rube's Waterloo.

I hurried him into the dressing room and kept close to him. He looked like a man who had lost the one thing worth while in his life. I turned a deaf ear to my players, to everybody, and hustled the Rube out and to the hotel. I wanted to be near him that night.

To my amaze we met Milly and Nan as we entered

the lobby. Milly wore a sweet, sympathetic smile. Nan shone more radiant than ever. I simply stared. It was Milly who got us all through the corridor into the parlor. I heard Nan talking.

"Whit, you pitched a bad game but—" there was the old teasing, arch, coquettishness—"but you are the best pitcher!"

"Nan!"

"Yes!"

The Rube's Honeymoon

He's got a new manager. Watch him pitch now!" That was what Nan Brown said to me about Rube Hurtle, my great pitcher, and I took it as her way of announcing her engagement.

My baseball career held some proud moments, but this one, wherein I realized the success of my matchmaking plans, was certainly the proudest one. So, entirely outside of the honest pleasure I got out of the Rube's happiness, there was reason for me to congratulate myself. He was a transformed man, so absolutely renewed, so wild with joy, that on the strength of it, I decided the pennant for Worcester was a foregone conclusion, and, sure of the money promised me by the directors, Milly and I began to make plans for the cottage upon the hill.

The Rube insisted on pitching Monday's game against the Torontos, and although poor fielding gave them a couple of runs, they never had a chance. They could not see the ball. The Rube wrapped it around their necks and between their wrists and straight over the plate with such incredible speed that they might just as well have tried to bat rifle bullets.

That night I was happy. Spears, my veteran captain,

was one huge smile; Radbourne quietly assured me that all was over now but the shouting; all the boys were happy.

And the Rube was the happiest of all. At the hotel he burst out with his exceeding good fortune. He and Nan were to be married upon the Fourth of July!

After the noisy congratulations were over and the Rube had gone, Spears looked at me and I looked at him.

"Con," said he soberly, "we just can't let him get married on the Fourth."

"Why not? Sure we can. We'll help him get married. I tell you it'll save the pennant for us. Look how he pitched today! Nan Brown is our salvation!"

"See here, Con, you've got softenin' of the brain, too. Where's your baseball sense? We've got a pennant to win. By July Fourth we'll be close to the lead again, an' there's that three weeks' trip on the road, the longest an' hardest of the season. We've just got to break even on that trip. You know what that means. If the Rube marries Nan—what are we goin' to do? We can't leave him behind. If he takes Nan with us—why it'll be a honeymoon! An' half the gang is stuck on Nan Brown! An' Nan Brown would flirt in her bridal veil! Why Con, we're up against a worse proposition than ever."

"Good Heavens! Cap. You're right," I groaned. "I never thought of that. We've got to postpone the wedding. . . . How on earth can we? I've heard her tell Milly that. She'll never consent to it. Say, this'll drive me to drink."

"All I got to say is this, Con. If the Rube takes his wife on that trip it's goin' to be an all-fired hummer. Don't you forget that."

"I'm not likely to. But, Spears, the point is this—will the Rube win his games?"

"Figurin' from his work today, I'd gamble he'll never lose another game. It ain't that. I'm thinkin' of what the gang will do to him an' Nan on the cars an' at the hotels. Oh! Lord, Con, it ain't possible to stand for that honeymoon trip! Just think!"

"If the worst comes to the worst, Cap, I don't care for anything but the games. If we get in the lead and stay there I'll stand for anything. . . . Couldn't the gang be coaxed or bought off to let the Rube and Nan alone?"

"Not on your life! There ain't enough love or money on earth to stop them. It'll be awful. Mind, I'm not responsible. Don't you go holdin' me responsible. In all my years of baseball I never went on a trip with a bride in the game. That's new on me, an' I never heard of it. It'd be bad enough if he wasn't a rube an' if she wasn't a crazy girl-fan an' a flirt to boot, an' with half the boys in love with her, but as it is—"

Spears gave up and, gravely shaking his head, he left me. I spent a little while in sober reflection, and finally came to the conclusion that, in my desperate ambition to win the pennant, I would have taken half a dozen rube pitchers and their baseball-made brides on the trip, if by so doing I could increase the percentage of games won. Nevertheless, I wanted to postpone the Rube's wedding if it was possible, and I went out to see Milly and asked her to help us. But for once in her life Milly turned traitor.

"Connie, you don't want to postpone it. Why, how perfectly lovely! Mrs. Stringer will go on that trip and Mrs. Bogart. . . . Connie, I'm going too!"

She actually jumped up and down in glee. That was the woman in her. It takes a wedding to get a woman. I remonstrated and pleaded and commanded, all to no purpose. Milly intended to go on that trip to see the games, and the fun, and the honeymoon.

She coaxed so hard that I yielded. Thereupon she called up Mrs. Stringer on the telephone, and of course found that young woman just as eager as she was. For my part, I threw anxiety and care to the four winds, and decided to be as happy as any of them. The pennant was mine! Something kept ringing that in my ears. With the Rube working his iron arm for the edification of his proud Nancy Brown, there was extreme likelihood of divers shutouts and humiliating defeats for some Eastern League teams.

How well I calculated became a matter of baseball history during that last week of June. We won six straight games, three of which fell to the Rube's credit. His opponents scored four runs in the three games, against the nineteen we made. Upon July 1, Radbourne beat Providence and Cairns won the second game. We now had a string of eight victories. Sunday we rested, and Monday was the Fourth, with morning and afternoon games with Buffalo.

Upon the morning of the Fourth, I looked for the Rube at the hotel, but could not find him. He did not show up at the grounds when the other boys did, and I began to worry. It was the Rube's turn to pitch and we were neck and neck with Buffalo for first place. If we won both games we would go ahead of our rivals. So I was all on edge, and kept going to the dressing room to see if the Rube had arrived. He came, finally, when all the boys were dressed, and about to go out for practice. He had on a new suit, a tailor-made suit at that, and he looked fine. There was about him a kind of strange radiance. He stated simply that he had arrived late because he had just been married. Before congratulations were out of our mouths, he turned to me.

"Con, I want to pitch both games today," he said.

"What! Say, Whit, Buffalo is on the card today and we are only three points behind them. If we win both we'll be leading the league once more. I don't know about pitching you both games."

"I reckon we'll be in the lead tonight then," he replied, "for I'll win them both."

I was about to reply when Dave, the groundkeeper, called me to the door, saying there was a man to see me. I went out, and there stood Morrisey, manager of the Chicago American League team. We knew each other well and exchanged greetings.

"Con, I dropped off to see you about this new pitcher of yours, the one they call the Rube. I want to see him work. I've heard he's pretty fast. How about it?"

"Wait—till you see him pitch," I replied. I could scarcely get that much out, for Morrisey's presence meant a great deal and I did not want to betray my elation.

"Any strings on him?" queried the big league manager, sharply.

"Well, Morrisey, not exactly. I can give you the first call. You'll have to bid high, though. Just wait till you see him work."

"I'm glad to hear that. My scout was over here watching him pitch and says he's a wonder."

What luck it was that Morrisey should have come upon this day! I could hardly contain myself. Almost I began to spend the money I would get for selling the Rube to the big league manager. We took seats in the grandstand, as Morrisey did not want to be seen by any players, and I stayed there with him until the gong sounded. There was a big attendance. I looked all over the stand for Nan, but she was lost in the gay crowd. But when I went down to the bench I saw her up in my private box with Milly. It took no second glance to see that Nan Brown was a bride and glorying in the fact.

Then, in the absorption of the game, I became oblivious to Milly and Nan; the noisy crowd; the giant firecrackers and the smoke; to the presence of Morrisey; to all except the Rube and my team and their opponents. Fortunately for my hopes, the game opened with characteristic Worcester dash. Little McCall doubled, Ashwell drew his base on four wide pitches, and Stringer drove the ball over the right-field fence—three runs!

Three runs were enough to win that game. Of all the exhibitions of pitching with which the Rube had favored us, this one was the finest. It was perhaps not so much his marvelous speed and unhittable curves that made the game one memorable in the annals of pitching; it was his perfect control in the placing of balls, in the cutting of corners; in his absolute implacable mastery of the situation. Buffalo was unable to find him at all. The game was swift, short, decisive, with the score 5 to 0 in our favor. But the score did not tell all of the Rube's work that morning. He shut out Buffalo without a hit, or a scratch, the first no-hit, no-run game of the year. He gave no base on balls; not a Buffalo player got to first base; only one fly went to the outfield.

For once I forgot Milly after a game, and I hurried to find Morrisey, and carried him off to have dinner with me.

"Your rube is a wonder, and that's a fact," he said to me several times. "Where on earth did you get him? Connelly, he's my meat. Do you understand? Can you let me have him right now?"

"No, Morrisey, I've got the pennant to win first. Then I'll sell him."

"How much? Do you hear? How much?" Morrisey hammered the table with his fist and his eyes gleamed.

Carried away as I was by his vehemence, I was yet able to calculate shrewdly, and I decided to name a very high price, from which I could come down and still make a splendid deal.

"How much?" demanded Morrisey.

"Five thousand dollars," I replied, and gulped when I got the words out.

Morrisey never batted an eye.

"Waiter, quick, pen and ink and paper!"

Presently my hand, none too firm, was signing my name to a contract whereby I was to sell my pitcher for five thousand dollars at the close of the current season. I never saw a man look so pleased as Morrisey when he folded that contract and put it in his pocket. He bade me goodbye and hurried off to catch a train, and he never knew the Rube had pitched the great game on his wedding day.

That afternoon before a crowd that had to be roped off the diamond, I put the Rube against the Bisons. How well he showed the baseball knowledge he had assimilated! He changed his style in that second game. He used a slow ball and wide curves and took things easy. He made Buffalo hit the ball and when runners got on bases once more let out his speed and held them down. He relied upon the players behind him and they were equal to the occasion.

It was a totally different game from that of the morning, and perhaps one more suited to the pleasure of the audience. There was plenty of hard hitting, sharp fielding, and good base running, and the game was close and exciting up to the eighth, when Mullaney's triple gave us two runs, and a lead that was not headed. To the deafening roar of the bleachers the Rube walked off the field, having pitched Worcester into first place in the pennant race.

That night the boys planned their first job on the Rube. We had ordered a special Pullman for travel to Toronto, and when I got to the depot in the morning, the Pullman was a white fluttering mass of satin ribbons. Also, there was a brass band, and thousands of baseball fans, and barrels of old footgear. The Rube and Nan arrived in a cab and were immediately mobbed. The crowd roared, the band played, the engine whistled, the bell clanged; and the air was full of confetti and slippers, and showers of rice like hail pattered everywhere. A somewhat disheveled bride and groom boarded the Pullman and breathlessly hid in a stateroom. The train started, and the crowd gave one last rousing cheer. Old Spears yelled from the back platform:

"Fellers, an' fans, you needn't worry none about leavin' the Rube an' his bride to the tender mercies of the gang. A hundred years from now people will talk about this honeymoon baseball trip. Wait till we come back—an' say, jest to put you wise, no matter what else happens, we're comin' back in first place!"

It was surely a merry party in that Pullman. The bridal couple emerged from their hiding place and held a sort of reception in which the Rube appeared shy and frightened, and Nan resembled a joyous, fluttering bird in gray. I did not see if she kissed every man on the team, but she kissed me as if she had been wanting to do it for ages. Milly kissed the Rube, and so did the other women, to his infinite embarrassment. Nan's effect upon that crowd was most singular. She was sweetness and caprice and joy personified.

We settled down presently to something approaching order, and I, for one, with very keen ears and alert eyes, because I did not want to miss anything.

"I see the lambs a-gambolin'," observed McCall, in a voice louder than was necessary to convey his meaning to Mullaney, his partner in the seat.

"Yes, it do seem as if there was joy a boundin' here-abouts," replied Mul with fervor.

"It's more springtime than summer," said Ashwell, "an' everything in nature is runnin' in pairs. There are the sheep an' the cattle an' the birds. I see two kingfishers fishin' over here. An' there's a couple of honeybees makin' honey. Oh, honey, an' by George, if there ain't two butterflies foldin' their wings round each other. See the dandelions kissin' in the field!"

Then the staid Captain Spears spoke up with an ap-

pearance of sincerity and a tone that was nothing short of
remarkable.

"Reggie, see the sunshine asleep upon yon bank.
Ain't it lovely? An' that white cloud sailin' thither amid
the blue—how spontaneous! Joy is abroad o'er all this
boo-tiful land today—Oh, yes! An' love's wings hover o'er
the little lambs an' the bullfrogs in the pond an' the dicky
birds in the trees. What sweetness to lie in the grass, the
lap of bounteous earth, eatin' apples in the Garden of
Eden, an' chasin' away the snakes an' dreamin' of Thee,
Sweet-h-e-a-r-t—"

Spears was singing when he got so far and there was
no telling what he might have done if Mullaney, unable
to stand the agony, had not jabbed a pin in him. But that
only made way for the efforts of the other boys, each of
whom tried to outdo the other in poking fun at the Rube
and Nan. The big pitcher was too gloriously happy to note
much of what went on around him, but when it dawned
upon him he grew red and white by turns.

Nan, however, was more than equal to the occasion.
Presently she smiled at Spears, such a smile! The captain
looked as if he had just partaken of an intoxicating wine.
With a heightened color in her cheeks and a dangerous
flash in her roguish eyes, Nan favored McCall with a look,
which was as much as to say that she remembered him
with a dear sadness. She made eyes at every fellow in the
car, and then bringing back her gaze to the Rube, as if
glorying in comparison, she nestled her curly black head
on his shoulder. He gently tried to move her; but it was
not possible. Nan knew how to meet the ridicule of half a
dozen old lovers. One by one they buried themselves in
newspapers, and finally McCall, for once utterly beaten,
showed a white feather, and sank back out of sight behind
his seat.

The boys did not recover from that shock until late in
the afternoon. As it was a physical impossibility for Nan to

rest her head all day upon her husband's broad shoulder, the boys toward dinnertime came out of their jealous trance. I heard them plotting something. When dinner was called, about half of my party, including the bride and groom, went at once into the dining car. Time there flew by swiftly. And later, when we were once more in our Pullman, and I had gotten interested in a game of cards with Milly and Stringer and his wife, the Rube came marching up to me with a very red face.

"Con, I reckon some of the boys have stolen my—our grips," said he.

"What?" I asked, blankly.

He explained that during his absence in the dining car someone had entered his stateroom and stolen his grip and Nan's. I hastened at once to aid the Rube in his search. The boys swore by everything under and beyond the sun they had not seen the grips; they appeared very much grieved at the loss and pretended to help in searching the Pullman. At last, with the assistance of a porter, we discovered the missing grips in an upper berth. The Rube carried them off to his stateroom and we knew soon from his uncomplimentary remarks that the contents of the suitcases had been mixed and manhandled. But he did not hunt for the jokers.

We arrived at Toronto before daylight next morning, and remained in the Pullman until seven o'clock. When we got out, it was discovered that the Rube and Nan had stolen a march upon us. We traced them to the hotel, and found them at breakfast. After breakfast we formed a merry sightseeing party and rode all over the city.

That afternoon, when Raddy let Toronto down with three hits and the boys played a magnificent game behind him, and we won 7 to 2, I knew at last and for certain that the Worcester team had come into its own again. Then next day Cairns won a close, exciting game, and following that, on the third day, the matchless Rube toyed with the Torontos. Eleven straight games won! I was in the clouds, and never had I seen so beautiful a light as shone in Milly's eyes.

From that day The Honeymoon Trip of the Worcester Baseball Club, as the newspapers heralded it—was a triumphant march. We won two out of three games at Montreal, broke even with the hard-fighting Bisons, took three straight from Rochester, and won one and tied one out of three with Hartford. It would have been wonderful ball playing for a team to play on home grounds and we were doing the full circuit of the league.

Spears had called the turn when he said the trip would be a hummer. Nan Hurtle had brought us wonderful luck.

But the tricks they played on Whit and his girl-fan bride!

Ashwell, who was a capital actor, disguised himself as a conductor and pretended to try to eject Whit and Nan from the train, urging that lovemaking was not permitted. Some of the team hired a clever young woman to hunt the Rube up at the hotel, and claim old acquaintance with him. Poor Whit almost collapsed when the young woman threw her arms about his neck just as Nan entered the parlor. Upon the instant Nan became wild as a little tigress, and it took much explanation and eloquence to reinstate Whit in her affections.

Another time Spears, the wily old fox, succeeded in detaining Nan on the way to the station, and the two missed the train. At first the Rube laughed with the others, but when Stringer remarked that he had noticed a growing attachment between Nan and Spears, my great pitcher experienced the first pangs of the green-eyed monster. We had to hold him to keep him from jumping from the train, and it took Milly and Mrs. Stringer to soothe him. I had to wire back to Rochester for a special train for Spears and Nan, and even then we had to play half a game without the services of our captain.

So far upon our trip I had been fortunate in securing comfortable rooms and the best of transportation for my party. At Hartford, however, I encountered difficulties. I could not get a special Pullman, and the sleeper we entered already had a number of occupants. After the ladies of my party had been assigned to berths, it was necessary for some of the boys to sleep double in upper berths.

It was late when we got aboard, the berths were already made up, and soon we had all retired. In the morning very early I was awakened by a disturbance. It sounded like a squeal. I heard an astonished exclamation, another squeal, the pattering of little feet, then hoarse uproar of laughter from the ball players in the upper berths. Following that came low, excited conversation between the porter and somebody, then an angry snort from the Rube and the thud of his heavy feet in the aisle. What took place after that was guesswork for me. But I gathered from the roars and bawls that the Rube was after some of the boys. I poked my head between the curtains and saw him digging into the berths.

"Where's McCall?" he yelled.

Mac was nowhere in that sleeper, judging from the vehement denials. But the Rube kept on digging and prodding in the upper berths.

"I'm a-goin' to lick you, Mac, so I reckon you'd better show up," shouted the Rube.

The big fellow was mad as a hornet. When he got to me he grasped me with his great fence-rail splitting hands and I cried out with pain.

"Say! Whit, let up! Mac's not here. . . . What's wrong?"

"I'll show you when I find him." And the Rube stalked on down the aisle, a tragically comic figure in his pajamas. In his search for Mac he pried into several upper

berths that contained occupants who were not ball players, and these protested in affright. Then the Rube began
to investigate the lower berths. A row of heads protruded
in a bobbing line from between the curtains of the upper
berths.

"Here, you Indian! Don't you look in there! That's
my wife's berth!" yelled Stringer.

Bogart, too, evinced great excitement.

"Hurtle, keep out of lower eight or I'll kill you," he
shouted.

What the Rube might have done there was no telling,
but as he grasped a curtain, he was interrupted by a
shriek from some woman assuredly not of our party.

"Get out! you horrid wretch! Help! Porter! Help!
Conductor!"

Instantly there was a deafening tumult in the car.
When it had subsided somewhat, and I considered I
would be safe, I descended from my berth and made my
way to the dressing room. Sprawled over the leather seat
was the Rube pommelling McCall with hearty goodwill. I
would have interfered, had it not been for Mac's demeanor. He was half frightened, half angry, and utterly
unable to defend himself or even resist, because he was
laughing, too.

"Doggone it! Whit—I didn't—do it! I swear it was
Spears! Stop thumpin' me now—or I'll get sore. . . . You
hear me! It wasn't me, I tell you. Cheese it!"

For all his protesting Mac received a good thumping,
and I doubted not in the least that he deserved it. The
wonder of the affair, however, was the fact that no one
appeared to know what had made the Rube so furious.
The porter would not tell, and Mac was strangely reticent,
though his smile was one to make a fellow exceedingly
sure something out of the ordinary had befallen. It was
not until I was having breakfast in Providence that I

learned the true cause of Rube's conduct, and Milly confided it to me, insisting on strict confidence.

"I promised not to tell," she said. "Now you promise you'll never tell."

"Well, Connie," went on Milly, when I had promised, "it was the funniest thing yet, but it was horrid of McCall. You see, the Rube had upper seven and Nan had lower seven. Early this morning, about daylight, Nan awoke very thirsty and got up to get a drink. During her absence, probably, but anyway sometime last night, McCall changed the number on her curtain, and when Nan came back to number seven of course she almost got in the wrong berth."

"No wonder the Rube punched him!" I declared. "I wish we were safe home. Something'll happen yet on this trip."

I was faithful to my promise to Milly, but the secret leaked out somewhere; perhaps Mac told it, and before the game that day all the players knew it. The Rube, having recovered his good humor, minded it not in the least. He could not have felt ill will for any length of time. Everything seemed to get back into smooth running order, and the Honeymoon Trip bade fair to wind up beautifully.

But, somehow or other, and about something unknown to the rest of us, the Rube and Nan quarreled. It was their first quarrel. Milly and I tried to patch it up but failed.

We lost the first game to Providence and won the second. The next day, a Saturday, was the last game of the trip, and it was Rube's turn to pitch. Several times during the first two days the Rube and Nan about half made up their quarrel, only in the end to fall deeper into it. Then the last straw came in a foolish move on the part of wilful Nan. She happened to meet Henderson, her former admirer, and in a flash she took up her flirtation with him where she had left off.

"Don't go to the game with him, Nan," I pleaded. "It's a silly thing for you to do. Of course you don't mean anything, except to torment Whit. But cut it out. The gang will make him miserable and we'll lose the game. There's no telling what might happen."

"I'm supremely indifferent to what happens," she replied, with a rebellious toss of her black head. "I hope Whit gets beaten."

She went to the game with Henderson and sat in the grandstand, and the boys spied them out and told the Rube. He did not believe it at first, but finally saw them, looked deeply hurt and offended, and then grew angry. But the gong, sounding at that moment, drew his attention to his business of the day, to pitch.

His work that day reminded me of the first game he ever pitched for me, upon which occasion Captain Spears got the best out of him by making him angry. For several innings Providence was helpless before his delivery. Then something happened that showed me a crisis was near. A wag of a fan yelled from the bleachers.

"Honeymoon Rube!"

This cry was taken up by the delighted fans and it rolled around the field. But the Rube pitched on, harder than ever. Then the knowing bleacherite who had started the cry changed it somewhat.

"Nanny's Rube!" he yelled.

This, too, went the rounds, and still the Rube, though red in the face, preserved his temper and his pitching control. All would have been well if Bud Wiler, comedian of the Providence team, had not hit upon a way to rattle Rube.

"Nanny's Goat!" he shouted from the coaching lines. Every Providence player took it up.

The Rube was not proof against that. He yelled so fiercely at them, and glared so furiously, and towered so formidably, that they ceased for the moment. Then he let drive with his fast straight ball and hit the first Providence batter in the ribs. His comrades had to help him to the bench. The Rube hit the next batter on the leg, and judging from the crack of the ball, I fancied that player would walk lame for several days. The Rube tried to hit the next batter and sent him to first on balls. Thereafter it became a dodging contest with honors about equal between pitcher and batters. The Providence players stormed and the bleachers roared. But I would not take the Rube out and the game went on with the Rube forcing in runs.

With the score a tie, and three men on bases one of the players on the bench again yelled: "Nanny's Goat!"

Straight as a string the Rube shot the ball at this fellow and bounded after it. The crowd rose in an uproar. The base runners began to score. I left my bench and ran across the space, but not in time to catch the Rube. I saw him hit two or three of the Providence men. Then the policemen got to him, and a real fight brought the big audience into the stamping melee. Before the Rube was collared I saw at least four blue-coats on the grass.

The game broke up, and the crowd spilled itself in streams over the field. Excitement ran high. I tried to force my way into the mass to get at the Rube and the officers, but this was impossible. I feared the Rube would be taken from the officers and treated with violence, so I waited with the surging crowd, endeavoring to get nearer. Soon we were in the street, and it seemed as if all the stands had emptied their yelling occupants.

A trolley car came along down the street, splitting the mass of people and driving them back. A dozen policemen summarily bundled the Rube upon the rear end of the car. Some of these officers boarded the car, and some remained in the street to beat off the vengeful fans.

I saw someone thrust forward a frantic young woman. The officers stopped her, then suddenly helped her on the car, just as I started. I recognized Nan. She gripped the Rube with both hands and turned a white, fearful face upon the angry crowd.

The Rube stood in the grasp of his wife and the policemen, and he looked like a ruffled lion. He shook his big fist and bawled in far-reaching voice:

"I can lick you all!"

To my infinite relief, the trolley gathered momentum and safely passed out of danger. The last thing I made out was Nan pressing close to the Rube's side. That moment saw their reconciliation and my joy that it was the end of the Rube's Honeymoon.

The Rube's Pennant

FELLOWS, it's this way. You've got to win today's game.
It's the last of the season and means the pennant
for Worcester. One more hard scrap and we're done! Of
all the uphill fights any bunch ever made to land the flag,
our has been the best. You're the best team I ever managed, the gamest gang of ball players that ever stepped in
spikes. We've played in the hardest kind of luck all season, except that short trip we called the Rube's Honeymoon. We got a bad start, and sore arms, and busted
fingers, all kinds of injuries, every accident calculated to
hurt a team's chances, came our way. But in spite of it all
we got the lead and we've held it, and today we're still a
few points ahead of Buffalo."

I paused to catch my breath, and looked round on the
grim, tired faces of my players. They made a stern group.
The close of the season found them almost played out.
What a hard chance it was, after their extraordinary efforts, to bring the issue of the pennant down to this last
game!

"If we lose today, Buffalo, with three games more to
play at home, will pull the bunting," I went on. "But
they're not going to win! I'm putting it up to you that

way. I know Spears is all in; Raddy's arm is gone; Ash is playing on one leg; you're all crippled. But you've got one more game in you, I know. These last few weeks the Rube has been pitching out of turn and he's about all in, too. He's kept us in the lead. If he wins today it'll be Rube's Pennant. But that might apply to all of you. Now, shall we talk over the play today? Any tricks to pull off? Any inside work?"

"Con, you're pretty much upset an' nervous," replied Spears, soberly. "It ain't no wonder. This has been one corker of a season. I want to suggest that you let me run the team today. I've talked over the play with the fellers. We ain't goin' to lose this game, Con. Buffalo has been comin' with a rush lately, an' they're confident. But we've been holdin' in, restin' up as much as we dared an' still keep our lead. Mebbee it'll surprise you to know we've bet every dollar we could get hold of on this game. Why, Buffalo money is everywhere."

"All right, Spears, I'll turn the team over to you. We've got the banner crowd of the year out there right now, a great crowd to play before. I'm more fussed up over this game than any I remember. But I have a sort of blind faith in my team. . . . I guess that's all I want to say."

Spears led the silent players out of the dressing room and I followed; and while they began to toss balls to and fro, to limber up cold, dead arms, I sat on the bench.

The Bisons were prancing about the diamond, and their swaggering assurance was not conducive to hope for the Worcesters. I wondered how many of that vast, noisy audience, intent on the day's sport, even had a thought of what pain and toil it meant to my players. The Buffalo men were in good shape; they had been lucky; they were at the top of their stride, and that made all the difference.

At any rate, there were a few faithful little women in the grandstand—Milly and Nan and Rose Stringer and

Kate Bogart—who sat with compressed lips and hoped and prayed for that game to begin and end.

The gong called off the practice, and Spears, taking the field, yelled gruff encouragement to his men. Umpire Carter brushed off the plate and tossed a white ball to Rube and called: "Play!" The bleachers set up an exultant, satisfied shout and sat down to wait.

Schultz toed the plate and watched the Rube pitch a couple. There seemed to be no diminution of the great pitcher's speed and both balls cut the plate. Schultz clipped the next one down the third-base line. Bogart trapped it close to the bag, and got it away underhand, beating the speedy runner by a nose. It was a pretty play to start with, and the spectators were not close-mouthed in appreciation. The short, stocky Carl ambled up to bat, and I heard him call the Rube something. It was not a friendly contest, this deciding game between Buffalo and Worcester.

"Bing one close to his swelled nut!" growled Spears to the Rube.

Carl chopped a bouncing grounder through short and Ash was after it like a tiger, but it was a hit. The Buffalo contingent opened up. Then Manning faced the Rube, and he, too, vented sarcasm. It might not have been heard by the slow, imperturbable pitcher for all the notice he took. Carl edged off first, slid back twice, got a third start, and on the Rube's pitch was off for second base with the lead that always made him dangerous. Manning swung vainly, and Gregg snapped a throw to Mullaney. Ball and runner got to the bag apparently simultaneously; the umpire called Carl out, and the crowd uttered a quick roar of delight.

The next pitch to Manning was a strike. Rube was not wasting any balls, a point I noted with mingled fear and satisfaction. For he might have felt that he had no strength to spare that day and so could not try to work the batters. Again he swung, and Manning rapped a long line fly over McCall. As the little left fielder turned at the sound of the hit and sprinted out, his lameness was certainly not in evidence. He was the swiftest runner in the league and always when he got going the crowd rose in wild clamor to watch him. Mac took that fly right off the foul flag in deep left, and the bleachers dinned their pleasure.

The teams changed positions. "Fellers," said Spears, savagely, "we may be a bunged-up lot of stiffs, but, say! We can hit! If you love your old captain—sting the ball!"

Vane, the Bison pitcher, surely had his work cut out for him. For one sympathetic moment I saw his part through his eyes. My Worcester veterans, long used to being under fire, were relentlessly bent on taking that game. It showed in many ways, particularly in their silence, because they were seldom a silent team. McCall hesitated a moment over his bats. Then, as he picked up the lightest one, I saw his jaw set, and I knew he intended to bunt. He was lame, yet he meant to beat out an infield hit. He went up scowling.

Vane had an old head, and he had a varied assortment of balls. For Mac he used an underhand curve, rising at the plate and curving in to the left-hander. Mac stepped back and let it go.

"That's the place, Bo," cried the Buffalo infielders. "Keep 'em close on the Crab." Eager and fierce as McCall was, he let pitch after pitch go by till he had three balls and two strikes. Still the heady Vane sent up another pitch similar to the others. Mac stepped forward in the box, dropped his bat on the ball, and leaped down the line toward first base. Vane came rushing in for the bunt, got it and threw. But as the speeding ball neared the baseman, Mac stretched out into the air and shot for the bag. By a fraction of a second he beat the ball. It was one of his demon-slides. He knew that the chances favored his being crippled; we all knew that some day Mac would slide recklessly once too often. But that, too, is all in the game and in the spirit of a great player.

"We're on," said Spears; "now keep with him."

By that the captain meant that Mac would go down, and Ashwell would hit with the run.

When Vane pitched, little McCall was flitting toward second. The Bison shortstop started for the bag, and Ash hit square through his tracks. A rolling cheer burst from the bleachers, and swelled till McCall overran third base and was thrown back by the coacher. Stringer hurried forward with his big bat.

"Oh! My!" yelled a fan, and he voiced my sentiments exactly. Here we would score, and be one run closer to that dearly bought pennant.

How well my men worked together! As the pitcher let the ball go, Ash was digging for second and Mac was shooting plateward. They played on the chance of Stringer's hitting. Stringer swung, the bat cracked, we heard a thud somewhere, and then Manning, half knocked over, was fumbling for the ball. He had knocked down a terrific drive with his mitt, and he got the ball in time to put Stringer out. But Mac scored and Ash drew a throw to third base and beat it. He had a bad ankle, but no one noticed it in that daring run.

"Watch me paste one!" said Captain Spears, as he spat several yards. He batted out a fly so long and high and far that, slow as he was, he had nearly run to second base when Carl made the catch. Ash easily scored on the throw-in. Then Bogart sent one skipping over second, and Treadwell, scooping it on the run, completed a play that showed why he was considered the star of the Bison infield.

"Two runs, fellers!" said Spears. "That's some! Push 'em over, Rube."

The second inning somewhat quickened the pace.

Even the Rube worked a little faster. Ellis lined to Cairns in right; Treadwell fouled two balls and had a called strike, and was out; McKnight hit a low fly over short, then Bud Wiler sent one between Spears and Mullaney. Spears went for it while the Rube with giant strides ran to cover first base. Between them they got Bud, but it was only because he was heavy and slow on his feet.

In our half of that inning Mullaney, Gregg, and Cairns went out in one, two, three order.

With Pannell up, I saw that the Rube held in on his speed, or else he was tiring. Pannell hit the second slow ball for two bases. Vane sacrificed, and then the redoubtable Schultz came up. He appeared to be in no hurry to bat. Then I saw that the foxy Buffalo players were working to tire the Rube. They had the situation figured. But they were no wiser than old Spears.

"Make 'em hit, Rube. Push 'em straight over. Never mind the corners. We don't care for a few runs. We'll hit this game out."

Shultz flied to Mac, who made a beautiful throw to the plate too late to catch Pannell. Carl deliberately bunted to the right of the Rube and it cost the big pitcher strenuous effort to catch his man.

"We got the Rube waggin'!" yelled a Buffalo player.

Manning tripled down the left foul line—a hit the bleachers called a screamer. When Ellis came up, it looked like a tie score, and when the Rube pitched it was plain that he was tired. The Bisons yelled their assurance of this and the audience settled into quiet. Ellis batted a scorcher that looked good for a hit. But the fast Ashwell was moving with the ball, and he plunged lengthwise to get it square in his glove. The hit had been so sharp that he had time to get up and make the throw to beat the runner. The bleachers thundered at the play.

"You're up, Rube," called Spears. "Lam one out of the lot!"

The Rube was an uncertain batter. There was never any telling what he might do, for he had spells of good and bad hitting. But when he did get his bat on the ball it meant a chase for some fielder. He went up swinging his huge club, and he hit a fly that would have been an easy home run for a fast man. But the best Rube could do was to reach third base. This was certainly good enough, as the bleachers loudly proclaimed, and another tally for us seemed sure.

McCall bunted toward third, another of his teasers. The Rube would surely have scored had he started with the ball, but he did not try and missed a chance. Wiler, of course, held the ball, and Mac got to first without special effort. He went down on the first pitch. Then Ash lined to Carl. The Rube waited till the ball was caught and started for home. The crowd screamed, the Rube ran for all he was worth and Carl's throw to the plate shot in low and true. Ellis blocked the Rube and tagged him out.

It looked to the bleachers as if Ellis had been unnecessarily rough, and they hissed and stormed disapproval. As for me, I knew the Bisons were losing no chance to wear out my pitcher. Stringer fouled out with Mac on third, and it made him so angry that he threw his bat toward the bench, making some of the boys skip lively.

The next three innings, as far as scoring was concerned, were all for Buffalo. But the Worcester infield played magnificent ball, holding their opponents to one run each inning.

That made the score 4 to 2 in favor of Buffalo.

In the last half of the sixth, with Ash on first base and two men out, old Spears hit another of his lofty flies, and this one went over the fence and tied the score. How the bleachers roared! It was full two minutes before they quieted down. To make it all the more exciting, Bogart hit safely, ran like a deer to third on Mullaney's grounder, which Wiler knocked down, and scored on a passed ball. Gregg ended the inning by striking out.

"Get at the Rube!" boomed Ellis, the Bison captain. "We'll have him up in the air soon. Get in the game now, you stickers!"

Before I knew what had happened, the Bisons had again tied the score. They were indomitable. They grew stronger all the time. A stroke of good luck now would clinch the game for them. The Rube was beginning to labor in the box; Ashwell was limping; Spears looked as if he would drop any moment; McCall could scarcely walk. But if the ball came his way he could still run. Nevertheless, I never saw any finer fielding than these crippled players executed that inning.

"Ash—Mac—can you hold out?" I asked, when they limped in. I received glances of scorn for my question. Spears, however, was not sanguine.

"I'll stick pretty much if somethin' doesn't happen," he said; "but I'm all in. I'll need a runner if I get to first this time."

Spears lumbered down to first base on an infield hit and the heavy Manning gave him the hip. Old Spears went down, and I for one knew he was out in more ways than that signified by Carter's sharp: "Out!"

The old warhorse gathered himself up slowly and painfully, and with his arms folded and his jaw protruding, he limped toward the umpire.

"Did you call me out?" he asked, in a voice plainly audible to anyone on the field.

"Yes," snapped Carter.

"What for? I beat the ball, an' Mannin' played dirty with me—gave me the hip."

"I called you out."

"But I wasn't out!"

"Shut up now! Get off the diamond!" ordered Carter, peremptorily.

"What? Me? Say, I'm captain of this team. Can't I question a decision?"

"Not mine. Spears, you're delaying the game."

"I tell you it was a rotten decision," yelled Spears. The bleachers agreed with him.

Carter grew red in the face. He and Spears had before then met in field squabbles, and he showed it.

"Fifty dollars!"

"More! You cheapskate—you piker! More!"

"It's a hundred!"

"Put me out of the game!" roared Spears.

"You bet! Hurry now—skedaddle!"

"Rob-b-ber!" bawled Spears.

Then he labored slowly toward the bench, all red, and wet with perspiration, his demeanor one of outraged dignity. The great crowd, as one man, stood up and yelled hoarsely at Carter, and hissed and railed at him. When Spears got to the bench he sat down beside me as if in pain, but he was smiling.

"Con, I was all in, an' knowin' I couldn't play any longer, thought I'd try to scare Carter. Say, he was white in the face. If we play into a close decision now, he'll give it to us."

Bogart and Mullaney batted out in short order, and once more the aggressive Bisons hurried in for their turn. Spears sent Cairns to first base and Jones to right. The Rube lobbed up his slow ball. In that tight pinch he showed his splendid nerve. Two Buffalo players, over-anxious, popped up flies. The Rube kept on pitching the slow curve until it was hit safely. Then heaving his shoulders with all his might he got all the motion possible into his swing and let drive. He had almost all of his old speed, but it hurt me to see him work with such desperate effort. He struck Wiler out.

He came stooping into the bench, apparently deaf to the stunning round of applause. Every player on the team had a word for the Rube. There was no quitting in that bunch, and if I ever saw victory on the stern faces of ball players it was in that moment.

"We haven't opened up yet. Mebbee this is the in-nin'. If it ain't, the next is," said Spears.

With the weak end of the batting list up, there seemed little hope of getting a run on Vane that inning. He had so much confidence that he put the ball over for Gregg, who hit out of the reach of the infield. Again Vane sent up his straight ball, no doubt expecting Cairns to hit into a double play. But Cairns surprised Vane and every-body else by poking a safety past first base. The fans began to howl and pound and whistle.

The Rube strode to bat. The infield closed in for a bunt, but the Rube had no orders for that style of play. Spears had said nothing to him. Vane lost his nonchalance and settled down. He cut loose with all his speed. Rube stepped out, suddenly whirled, then tried to dodge, but the ball hit him fair in the back. Rube sagged in his tracks, then straightened up, and walked slowly to first base. Score 5 to 5, bases full, no outs, McCall at bat. I sat dumb on the bench, thrilling and shivering. McCall! Ashwell! Stringer to bat!

"Play it safe! Hold the bags!" yelled the coacher.

McCall fairly spouted defiance as he faced Vane.

"Pitch! It's all off! An' you know it!"

If Vane knew that, he showed no evidence of it. His face was cold, unsmiling, rigid. He had to pitch to McCall, the fastest man in the league; to Ashwell, the best bunter; to Stringer, the champion batter. It was a supreme test for a great pitcher. There was only one kind of a ball that McCall was not sure to hit, and that was a high curve, in close. Vane threw it with all his power. Carter called it a strike. Again Vane swung and his arm fairly cracked. Mac fouled the ball. The third was wide. Slowly, with lifting breast, Vane got ready, whirled savagely and shot up the ball. McCall struck out.

As the Buffalo players crowed and the audience groaned it was worthy of note that little McCall showed no temper. Yet he had failed to grasp a great opportunity.

"Ash, I couldn't see 'em," he said, as he passed to the bench. "Speed, whew! Look out for it. He's been savin' up. Hit quick, an' you'll get him."

Ashwell bent over the plate and glowered at Vane.

"Pitch! It's all off! An' you know it!" he hissed, using Mac's words.

Ashwell, too, was left-handed; he, too, was extremely hard to pitch to; and if he had a weakness that any of us ever discovered, it was a slow curve and change of pace. But I doubted if Vane would dare to use slow balls to Ash at that critical moment. I had yet to learn something of Vane. He gave Ash a slow, wide-sweeping sidewheeler, that curved round over the plate. Ash always took a strike, so this did not matter. Then Vane used his deceptive change of pace, sending up a curve that just missed Ash's bat as he swung.

"Oh! Ahh! hit!" wailed the bleachers.

Vane doubled up like a contortionist, and shot up a lightning-swift drop that fooled Ash completely. Again the crowd groaned. Score tied, bases full, two out, Stringer at bat!

"It's up to you, String," called Ash, stepping aside.

Stringer did not call out to Vane. That was not his way. He stood tense and alert, bat on his shoulder, his powerful form braced, and he waited. The outfielders trotted over toward right field, and the infielders played deep, calling out warnings and encouragement to the pitcher. Stringer had no weakness, and Vane knew this. Nevertheless he did not manifest any uneasiness, and pitched the first ball without any extra motion. Carter called it a strike. I saw Stringer sink down slightly and grow tenser all over. I believe that moment was longer for me than for either the pitcher or the batter. Vane took his time, watched the base runners, feinted to throw to catch them, and then delivered the ball toward the plate with the limit of his power.

Stringer hit the ball. As long as I live, I will see that glancing low liner. Shultz, by a wonderful play in deep center, blocked the ball and thereby saved it from being a home run. But when Stringer stopped on second base, all the runners had scored.

A shrill, shrieking, high-pitched yell! The bleachers threatened to destroy the stands and also their throats in one long revel of baseball madness.

Jones, batting in place of Spears, had gone up and fouled out before the uproar had subsided.

"Fellers, I reckon I feel easier," said the Rube. It was the only time I had ever heard him speak to the players at such a stage.

"Only six batters, Rube," called out Spears. "Boys, it's a grand game, an' it's our'n!"

The Rube had enough that inning to dispose of the lower half of the Buffalo list without any alarming bids for a run. And in our half, Bogart and Mullaney hit vicious ground balls that gave Treadwell and Wiler opportunities for superb plays. Carl, likewise, made a beautiful running catch of Gregg's line fly. The Bisons were still in the game, still capable of pulling it out at the last moment.

When Shultz stalked up to the plate I shut my eyes a moment, and so still was it that the field and stands might have been empty. Yet, though I tried, I could not keep my eyes closed. I opened them to watch the Rube. I knew Spears felt the same as I, for he was blowing like a porpoise and muttering to himself: "Mebee the Rube won't last an' I've no one to put in!"

The Rube pitched with heavy, violent effort. He had

still enough speed to be dangerous. But after the manner of ball players Shultz and the coaches mocked him.

"Take all you can," called Ellis to Shultz.

Every pitch lessened the Rube's strength and these wise opponents knew it. Likewise the Rube himself knew, and never had he shown better head work than in this inning. If he were to win, he must be quick. So he wasted not a ball. The first pitch and the second, delivered breast high and fairly over the plate, beautiful balls to hit, Shultz watched speed by. He swung hard on the third and the crippled Ashwell dove for it in a cloud of dust, got a hand in front of it, but uselessly, for the hit was safe. The crowd cheered that splendid effort.

Carl marched to bat, and he swung his club over the plate as if he knew what to expect. "Come on, Rube!" he shouted. Wearily, doggedly, the Rube whirled, and whipped his arm. The ball had all his old glancing speed and it was a strike. The Rube was making a tremendous effort. Again he got his body in convulsive motion—two strikes! Shultz had made no move to run, nor had Carl made any move to hit. These veterans were waiting. The Rube had pitched five strikes—could he last?

"Now, Carl!" yelled Ellis, with startling suddenness, as the Rube pitched again.

Crack! Carl placed that hit as safely through short as if he had thrown it. McCall's little legs twinkled as he dashed over the grass. He had to head off that hit and he ran like a streak. Down and forward he pitched, as if in one of his fierce slides, and he got his body in front of the ball, blocking it, and then he rolled over and over. But he jumped up and lined the ball to Bogart, almost catching Shultz at third base. Then, as Mac tried to walk, his lame leg buckled under him, and down he went, and out.

"Call time," I called to Carter. "McCall is done. . . . Myers, you go to left an' for Lord's sake play ball!"

Stringer and Bogart hurried to Mac and, lifting him

up and supporting him between them with his arms around their shoulders, they led him off amid cheers from the stands. Mac was white with pain.

"Naw, I won't go off the field. Leave me on the bench," he said. "Fight 'em now. It's our game. Never mind a couple of runs."

The boys ran back to their positions and Carter called play. Perhaps a little delay had been helpful to the Rube. Slowly he stepped into the box and watched Shultz at third and Carl at second. There was not much probability of his throwing to catch them off the base, but enough of a possibility to make them careful, so he held them close.

The Rube pitched a strike to Manning, then another. That made eight strikes square over the plate that inning. What magnificent control! It was equaled by the implacable patience of those veteran Bisons. Manning hit the next ball as hard as Carl had hit his. But Mullaney plunged down, came up with the ball, feinted to fool Carl, then let drive to Gregg to catch the fleeting Shultz. The throw went wide, but Gregg got it, and, leaping lengthwise, tagged Shultz out a yard from the plate.

One out. Two runners on bases. The bleachers rose and split their throats. Would the inning never end?

Spears kept telling himself: "They'll score, but we'll win. It's our game!"

I had a sickening fear that the strange confidence that obsessed the Worcester players had been blind, unreasoning vanity.

"Carl will steal," muttered Spears. "He can't be stopped."

Spears had called the play. The Rube tried to hold the little base-stealer close to second, but, after one attempt, wisely turned to his hard task of making the Bisons hit and hit quickly. Ellis let the ball pass; Gregg made a perfect throw to third; Bogart caught the ball and moved like a flash, but Carl slid under his hands to the bag. Manning ran down to second. The Rube pitched again, and this was his tenth ball over the plate. Even the Buffalo players evinced eloquent appreciation of the Rube's defense at this last stand.

Then Ellis sent a clean hit to right, scoring both Carl and Manning. I breathed easier, for it seemed with those two runners in; the Rube had a better chance. Treadwell also took those two runners in; the Rube had a way those Bisons waited. They had their reward, for the Rube's speed left him. When he pitched again the ball had control, but no shoot. Treadwell hit it with all his strength. Like a huge cat Ashwell pounced upon it, ran over second base, forcing Ellis, and his speedy snap to first almost caught Treadwell.

Score 8 to 7. Two out. Runner on first. One run to tie.

In my hazy, dimmed vision I saw the Rube's pennant waving from the flagpole.

"It's our game!" howled Spears in my ear, for the noise from the stands was deafening. "It's our pennant!"

The formidable batting strength of the Bisons had been met, not without disaster, but without defeat. McKnight came up for Buffalo and the Rube took his weary swing. The batter made a terrific lunge and hit the ball with a solid crack. It lined for center.

Suddenly electrified into action, I leaped up. That hit! It froze me with horror. It was a home run. I saw Stringer fly toward left center. He ran like something wild. I saw the heavy Treadwell lumbering round the bases. I saw Ashwell run out into center field.

"Ahh!" The whole audience relieved its terror in that expulsion of suspended breath. Stringer had leaped high to knock down the ball, saving a sure home run and the game. He recovered himself, dashed back for the ball and shot it to Ash.

When Ash turned toward the plate, Treadwell was rounding third base. A tie score appeared inevitable. I saw

Ash's arm whip and the ball shoot forward, leveled, glancing, beautiful in its flight. The crowd saw it, and the silence broke to a yell that rose and rose as the ball sped in. That yell swelled to a splitting shriek, and Treadwell slid in the dust, and the ball shot into Gregg's hands all at the same instant.

Carter waved both arms upwards. It was the umpire's action when his decision went against the base runner. The audience rolled up one great stenorian cry.

"Out!"

I collapsed and sank back upon the bench. My confused senses received a dull roar of pounding feet and dinning voices as the herald of victory. I felt myself thinking how pleased Milly would be. I had a distinct picture in my mind of a white cottage on a hill, no longer a dream, but a reality, made possible for me by the Rube's winning of the pennant.

Breaking into
Fast Company

THEY may say baseball is the same in the minor
leagues as it is in the big leagues, but any old ball
player or manager knows better. Where the difference
comes in, however, is in the greater excellence and unity
of the major players, a speed, a daring, a finish that can be
acquired only in competition with one another.

I thought of this when I led my party into Morrisey's
private box in the grandstand of the Chicago American
League grounds. We had come to see the Rube's break
into fast company. My great pitcher, Whittaker Hurtle,
the Rube, as we called him, had won the Eastern League
Pennant for me that season, and Morrisey, the Chicago
magnate, had bought him. Milly, my affianced, was with
me, looking as happy as she was pretty, and she was
chaperoned by her mother, Mrs. Nelson.

With me, also, were two veterans of my team, McCall
and Spears, who lived in Chicago, and who would have
traveled a few miles to see the Rube pitch. And the other
member of my party was Mrs. Hurtle, the Rube's wife, as
saucy and as sparkling-eyed as when she had been Nan
Brown. Today she wore a new tailor-made gown, new

bonnet, new gloves—she said she had decorated herself in a manner befitting the wife of a major league pitcher.

Morrisey's box was very comfortable, and, as I was pleased to note, so situated that we had a fine view of the field and stands, and yet were comparatively secluded. The bleachers were filling. Some of the Chicago players were on the field tossing and batting balls; the Rube, however, had not yet appeared.

A moment later a metallic sound was heard on the stairs leading up into the box. I knew it for baseball spiked shoes clanking on the wood.

The Rube, looking enormous in his uniform, stalked into the box, knocking over two chairs as he entered. He carried a fielder's glove in one huge freckled hand, and a big black bat in the other.

Nan, with much dignity and a very manifest pride, introduced him to Mrs. Nelson.

There was a little chatting, and then, upon the arrival of Manager Morrisey, we men retired to the back of the box to talk baseball.

Chicago was in fourth place in the league race, and had a fighting chance to beat Detroit out for the third position. Philadelphia was scheduled for that day, and Philadelphia had a great team. It was leading the race, and almost beyond all question would land the flag. In truth, only one more victory was needed to clinch the pennant. The team had three games to play in Chicago and it was to wind up the season with three in Washington. Six games to play and only one imperatively important to win! But baseball is uncertain, and until the Philadelphians won that game they would be a band of fiends.

"Well, Whit, this is where you break in," I said. "Now, tip us straight. You've had more than a week's rest. How's that arm?"

"Grand, Con, grand!" replied the Rube with his frank

smile. "I was a little anxious till I warmed up. But say! I've got more up my sleeve today than I ever had."

"That'll do for me," said Morrisey, rubbing his hands. "I'll spring something on these swelled Quakers today. Now, Connelly, give Hurtle one of your old talks—the last one—and then I'll ring the gong."

I added some words of encouragement, not forgetting my old ruse to incite the Rube by rousing his temper. And then, as the gong rang and the Rube was departing, Nan stepped forward for her say. There was a little white under the tan on her cheek, and her eyes had a darkling flash.

"Whit, it's a magnificent sight—that beautiful green field and the stands. What a crowd of fans! Why, I never saw a real baseball crowd before. There are twenty thousand here. And there's a difference in the feeling. It's sharper—new to me. It's big league baseball. Not a soul in that crowd ever heard of you, but, I believe, tomorrow the whole baseball world will have heard of you. Mr. Morrisey knows. I saw it in his face. Captain Spears knows. Connie knows. I know."

Then she lifted her face and, pulling him down within reach, she kissed him. Nan took her husband's work in dead earnest; she gloried in it, and perhaps she had as much to do with making him a great pitcher as any of us.

The Rube left the box, and I found a seat between Nan and Milly. The field was a splendid sight. Those bleachers made me glow with managerial satisfaction. On the field both teams pranced and danced and bounced around in practice.

In spite of the absolutely last degree of egotism manifested by the Philadelphia players, I could not but admire such a splendid body of men.

"So these are the champions of last season and of this season, too," commented Milly. "I don't wonder. How swiftly and cleanly they play! They appear not to exert themselves, yet they always get the ball in perfect time. It all reminds me of—of the rhythm of music. And that champion batter and runner—that Lane in center—isn't he just beautiful? He walks and runs like a blue-ribbon winner at the horse show. I tell you one thing, Connie, these Quakers are on dress parade."

"Oh, these Quakers hate themselves, I don't think!" retorted Nan. Being a rabid girl-fan it was, of course, impossible for Nan to speak baseball convictions or gossip without characteristic baseball slang. "Stuck on themselves! I never saw the like in my life. That fellow Lane is so swelled that he can't get down off his toes. But he's a wonder, I must admit that. They're a bunch of stars. Easy, fast, trained—they're machines, and I'll bet they're Indians to fight. I can see it sticking out all over them. This will certainly be some game with Whit handing up that jump ball of his to this gang of champs. But, Connie, I'll go you Whit beats them."

I laughed and refused to gamble.

The gong rang; the crowd seemed to hum and rustle softly to quiet attention; Umpire McClung called the names of the batteries; then the familiar "Play!"

There was the usual applause from the grandstand and welcome cheers from the bleachers. The Rube was the last player to go out. Morrisey was a manager who always played to the stands, and no doubt he held the Rube back for effect. If so, he ought to have been gratified. That moment reminded me of my own team and audience upon the occasion of the Rube's debut. It was the same—only here it happened in the big league, before a championship team and twenty thousand fans.

The roar that went up from the bleachers might well have scared an unseasoned pitcher out of his wits. And the Quakers lined up before their bench and gazed at this newcomer who had the nerve to walk out there to the box. Cogswell stood on the coaching line, looked at the Rube and then held up both arms and turned toward the Chicago bench as if to ask Morrisey: "Where did you get that?"

Nan, quick as a flash to catch a point, leaned over the box-rail and looked at the champions with fire in her eye. "Oh, you just wait! wait!" she bit out between her teeth.

Certain it was that there was no one who knew the Rube as well as I; and I knew beyond the shadow of a doubt that the hour before me would see brightening of a great star pitcher on the big league horizon. It was bound to be a full hour for me. I had much reason to be grateful to Whit Hurtle. He had pulled my team out of a rut and won me the pennant, and the five thousand dollars I got for his release bought the little cottage on the hill for Milly and me. Then there was my pride in having developed him. And all that I needed to calm me, settle me down into assurance and keen criticism of the game, was to see the Rube pitch a few balls with his old incomparable speed and control.

Berne, first batter for the Quakers, walked up to the plate. He was another Billy Hamilton, built like a wedge. I saw him laugh at the long pitcher.

Whit swayed back, coiled and uncoiled. Something thin, white, glancing, shot at Berne. He ducked, escaping the ball by a smaller margin than appeared good for his confidence. He spoke low to the Rube, and what he said was probably not flavored with the milk of friendly sweetness.

"Wild! What'd you look for?" called out Cogswell scornfully. "He's from the woods!"

The Rube swung his enormously long arm, took an enormous stride toward third base, and pitched again. It was one of his queer deliveries. The ball cut the plate.

"Ho! Ho!" yelled the Quakers.

The Rube's next one was his out curve. It broke

toward the corner of the plate and would have been a strike had not Berne popped it up.

Callopy, the second hitter, faced the Rube, and he, too, after the manner of ball players, made some remark meant only for the Rube's ears. Callopy was a famous waiter. He drove more pitchers mad with his implacable patience than any hitter in the league. The first one of the Rube's he waited on crossed the in-corner; the second crossed the out-corner and the third was Rube's wide, slow, tantalizing "stitch-ball," as we call it, for the reason that it came so slow a batter could count the stitches. I believe Callopy waited on that curve, decided to hit it, changed his mind and waited some more, and finally the ball maddened him and he had to poke at it, the result being a weak grounder.

Then the graceful, powerful Lane, champion batter, champion base runner, stepped to the plate. How a baseball crowd, any crowd, anywhere, loves the champion batter! The ovation Lane received made me wonder, with this impressive reception in a hostile camp, what could be the manner of it on his home field? Any boy ballplayer from the lots seeing Lane knock the dirt out of his spikes and step into position would have known he was a .400 hitter.

I was curious to see what the Rube would pitch Lane. It must have been a new and significant moment for Hurtle. Some pitchers actually wilt when facing a hitter of Lane's reputation. But he, on his baseball side, was peculiarly unemotional. Undoubtedly he could get furious, but that only increased his effectiveness. To my amazement the Rube pitched Lane a little easy ball, not in any sense like his floater or stitch-ball, but just a little toss that any youngster might have tossed. Of all possible balls, Lane was not expecting such as that, and he let it go. If the nerve of it amazed me, what did it not do to Lane? I saw his face go fiery red. The grandstand murmured; let out one short yelp of pleasure; the Quaker players chaffed Lane.

The pitch was a strike. I was gripping my chair now, and for the next pitch I prophesied the Rube's wonderful jump ball, which he had not yet used. He swung long, and at the end of his swing seemed to jerk tensely. I scarcely saw the ball. It had marvelous speed. Lane did not offer to hit it, and it was a strike. He looked at the Rube, then at Cogswell. That veteran appeared amused. The bleachers, happy and surprised to be able to yell at Lane, yelled heartily.

Again I took it upon myself to interpret the Rube's pitching mind. He had another ball that he had not used, a drop, an unhittable drop. I thought he would use that next. He did, and though Lane reached it with the bat, the hit was a feeble one. He had been fooled and the side was out.

Poole, the best of the Quaker's pitching staff, walked out to the slab. He was a left-hander, and Chicago, having so many players who batted left-handed, always found a southpaw a hard nut to crack. Cogswell, field manager and captain of the Quakers, kicked up the dust around first base and yelled to his men: "Git in the game!"

Staats hit Poole's speed ball into deep short and was out; Mitchell flew out to Berne; Rand grounded to second.

While the teams again changed sides the fans cheered, and then indulged in the first stretch of the game. I calculated that they would be stretching their necks presently, trying to keep track of the Rube's work. Nan leaned on the railing absorbed in her own hope and faith. Milly chattered about this and that, people in the boxes, and the chances of the game.

My own interest, while it did not wholly preclude the fortunes of the Chicago players at the bat, was mostly concerned with the Rube's fortunes in the field.

In the Rube's half inning he retired Bannister and Blandy on feeble infield grounders, and worked Cogswell into hitting a wide curve high in the air.

Poole meant to win for the Quakers if his good arm and cunning did not fail him, and his pitching was masterly. McCloskey fanned, Hutchinson fouled out, Brewster got a short safe fly just out of reach, and Hoffner hit to second, forcing Brewster.

With Dugan up for the Quakers in the third inning, Cogswell and Bannister, from the coaching lines, began to talk to the Rube. My ears, keen from long practice, caught some of the remarks in spite of the noisy bleachers.

"Say, busher, you've lasted longer'n we expected, but you don't know it!"

"Gol darn you city ball tossers! Now you jest let me alone!"

"We're comin' through the rye!"

"My top-heavy rustic friend, you'll need an airship presently, when you go up!"

All the badinage was good-natured, which was sure proof that the Quakers had not arrived at anything like real appreciation of the Rube. They were accustomed to observe the trying out of many youngsters, of whom ninety-nine out of a hundred failed to make good.

Dugan chopped at three strikes and slammed his bat down. Hucker hit a slow fly to Hoffer. Three men out on five pitched balls! Cogswell, old war horse that he was, stood a full moment and watched the Rube as he walked in to the bench. An idea had penetrated Cogswell's brain, and I would have given something to know what it was. Cogswell was a great baseball general, and though he had a preference for matured ballplayers he could, when pressed, see the quality in a youngster. He picked up his mitt and took his position at first with a gruff word to his players.

Rand for Chicago opened with a hit, and the bleachers, ready to strike fire, began to cheer and stamp. When McCloskey, in an attempt to sacrifice, beat out his bunt the crowd roared. Rand, being slow on his feet, had not attempted to make third on the play. Hutchinson sacrificed, neatly advancing the runners. Then the bleachers played the long rolling drum of clattering feet with shrill whistling accompaniment. Brewster batted a wicked ground ball to Blandy. He dove into the dust, came up with the ball, and feinting to throw home he wheeled and shot the ball to Cogswell, who in turn shot it to the plate to head Rand. Runner and ball got there apparently together, but Umpire McClung's decision went against Rand. It was fine, fast work, but how the bleachers stormed at McClung!

"Rob-b-ber!"

Again the head of the Quakers' formidable list was up. I knew from the way that Cogswell paced the coaching box that the word had gone out to look the Rube over seriously. There were possibilities even in rubes.

Berne carefully stepped into the batter's box, as if he wanted to be certain to the breadth of a hair how close he was to the plate. He was there this time to watch the Rube pitch, to work him out, to see what was what. He crouched low, and it would have been extremely hard to guess what he was up to. His great play, however, was his ability to dump the ball and beat out the throw to first. It developed presently, that this was now his intention and that the Rube knew it and pitched him the one ball which is almost impossible to bunt—a high incurve, over the inside corner. There was no mistaking the Rube's magnificent control. True as a plumb line he shot up the ball— once, twice, and Berne fouled both—two strikes. Grudgingly he waited on the next, but it, too, was over the corner, and Berne went out on strikes. The great crowd did not, of course, grasp the finesse of the play, but Berne had struck out—that was enough for them.

Callopy, the famous spiker, who had put many a player out of the game for weeks at a time, strode into the batter's place, and he, too, was not at the moment making any funny remarks. The Rube delivered a ball that all but hit Callopy fair on the head. It was the second narrow escape for him, and the roar he let out showed how he resented being threatened with a little of his own medicine. As might have been expected, and very likely as the Rube intended, Callopy hit the next ball, a sweeping curve, up over the infield.

I was trying to see all the intricate details of the motive and action on the field, and it was not easy to watch several players at once. But while Berne and Callopy were having their troubles with the Rube, I kept the tail of my eye on Cogswell. He was prowling up and down the third-base line.

He was missing no signs, no indications, no probabilities, no possibilities. But he was in doubt. Like a hawk he was watching the Rube, and, as well, the crafty batters. The inning might not tell the truth as to the Rube's luck, though it would test his control. The Rube's speed and curves, without any head work, would have made him a pitcher of no mean ability, but was this remarkable placing of balls just accident? That was the question.

When Berne walked to the bench I distinctly heard him say: "Come out of it, you dubs. I say you can't work him or wait him. He's peggin' 'em out of a gun!"

Several of the Quakers were standing out from the bench, all intent on the Rube. He had stirred them up. First it was humor; then ridicule, curiosity, suspicion, doubt. And I knew it would grow to wonder and certainty, then fierce attack from both tongues and bats, and lastly—for ball players are generous—unstinted admiration.

Somehow, not only the first climaxes of a game but the decisions, the convictions, the reputations of pitchers and fielders evolve around the great hitter. Plain it was that the vast throng of spectators, eager to believe in a new find, wild to welcome a new star, yet loath to trust to their own impulsive judgments, held themselves in check until once more the great Lane had faced the Rube.

The field grew tolerably quiet just then. The Rube did not exert himself. The critical stage had no concern for him. He pitched Lane a high curve, over the plate, but in close, a ball meant to be hit and a ball hard to hit safely. Lane knew that as well as any hitter in the world, so he let two of the curves go by—two strikes. Again the Rube relentlessly gave him the same ball; and Lane, hitting viciously, spitefully, because he did not want to hit that kind of a ball, sent up a fly that Rand easily captured.

"Oh, I don't know! Pretty fair, I guess!" yelled a tenor-voiced fan; and he struck the keynote. And the bleachers rose to their feet and gave the Rube the rousing cheer of the brotherhood of fans.

Hoffer walked to first on a base on balls. Sweeney advanced him. The Rube sent up a giant fly to Callopy. Then Staats hit safely, scoring the first run of the game. Hoffer crossed the plate amid vociferous applause. Mitchell ended the inning with a fly to Blandy.

What a change had come over the spirit of that Quaker aggregation! It was something to make a man thrill with admiration and, if he happened to favor Chicago, to fire all his fighting blood. The players poured upon the Rube a continuous stream of scathing abuse. They would have made a raging devil of a mild-mannered clergyman. Some of them were skilled in caustic wit, most of them were possessed of forked tongues; and Cogswell, he of a thousand baseball battles, had a genius for inflaming anyone he tormented. This was mostly beyond the ken of the audience, and behind the back of the umpire, but it was perfectly plain to me. The Quakers were trying to rattle the Rube, a trick of the game as fair for one side

as for the other. I sat there tight in my seat, grimly glorying in the way the Rube refused to be disturbed. But the
lion in him was rampant. Fortunately, it was his strange
gift to pitch better the angrier he got; and the more the
Quakers flayed him, the more he let himself out to their
crushing humiliation.

The innings swiftly passed to the eighth with Chicago
failing to score again, with Philadelphia failing to score at
all. One scratch hit and a single, gifts to the weak end of
the batting list, were all the lank pitcher allowed them.
Long since the bleachers had crowned the Rube. He was
theirs and they were his; and their voices had the peculiar
strangled hoarseness due to over-exertion. The grandstand, slower to understand and approve, arrived later;
but it got there about the seventh, and ladies' gloves and
men's hats were sacrificed.

In the eighth the Quakers reluctantly yielded their
meed of praise, showing it by a cessation of their savage
wordy attacks on the Rube. It was a kind of sullen respect,
wrung from the bosom of great foes.

Then the ninth inning was at hand. As the sides
changed I remembered to look at the feminine group in
our box. Milly was in a most beautiful glow of happiness
and excitement. Nan sat rigid, leaning over the rail, her
face white and drawn, and she kept saying in a low voice:
"Will it never end? Will it never end?" Mrs. Nelson stared
wearily.

It was the Quakers' last stand. They faced it as a team
that had won many a game in the ninth with two men
out. Dugan could do nothing with the Rube's unhittable
drop, for a drop curve was his weakness, and he struck
out. Hucker hit to Hoffer, who fumbled, making the first
error of the game. Poole dumped the ball, as evidently the
Rube desired, for he handed up a straight one, but the
bunt rolled teasingly and the Rube, being big and tall,
failed to field it in time.

Suddenly the whole field grew quiet. For the first time Cogswell's coaching was clearly heard.

"One out! Take a lead! Take a lead! Go through this time. Go through!"

Could it be possible, I wondered, that after such a wonderful exhibition of pitching the Rube would lose out in the ninth?

There were two Quakers on base, one out, and two of the best hitters in the league on deck, with a chance of Lane getting up.

"Oh! Oh! Oh!" moaned Nan.

I put my hand on hers. "Don't quit, Nan. You'll never forgive yourself if you quit. Take it from me, Whit will pull out of this hole!"

What a hole that was for the Rube on the day of his break into fast company! I measured it by his remarkable deliberation. He took a long time to get ready to pitch to Berne, and when he let drive it was as if he had been trifling all before in that game. I could think of no way to figure it except that when the ball left him there was scarcely any appreciable interval of time before it cracked in Sweeney's mitt. It was the Rube's drop, which I believed unhittable. Berne let it go by, shaking his head as McClung called it a strike. Another followed, which Berne chopped at vainly. Then with the same upheaval of his giant frame, the same flinging of long arms and lunging forward, the Rube delivered a third drop. And Berne failed to hit it.

The voiceless bleachers stamped on the benches and the grandstand likewise thundered.

Callopy showed his craft by stepping back and lining Rube's high pitch to left. Hoffer leaped across and plunged down, getting his gloved hand in front of the ball. The hit was safe, but Hoffer's valiant effort saved a tie score.

Lane up! Three men on bases! Two out!

Not improbably there were many thousand spectators

of that thrilling moment who pitied the Rube for the fate which placed Lane at the bat then. But I was not one of them. Nevertheless my throat was clogged, my mouth dry, and my ears full of bells. I could have done something terrible to Hurtle for his deliberation, yet I knew he was proving himself what I had always tried to train him to be.

Then he swung, stepped out, and threw his body with the ball. This was his rarely used pitch, his last resort, his fast rise ball that jumped up a little at the plate. Lane struck under it. How significant on the instant to see old Cogswell's hands go up! Again the Rube pitched, and this time Lane watched the ball go by. Two strikes!

That whole audience leaped to its feet, whispering, yelling, screaming, roaring, bawling.

The Rube received the ball from Sweeney and quick as lightning he sped it plateward. The great Lane struck out! The game was over—Chicago, 1; Philadelphia, 0.

In that whirling moment when the crowd went mad and Milly was hugging me, and Nan pounding holes in my hat, I had a queer sort of blankness, a section of time when my sensations were deadlocked.

"Oh! Connie, look!" cried Nan. I saw Lane and Cogswell warmly shaking hands with the Rube. Then the hungry clamoring fans tumbled upon the field and swarmed about the players.

Whereupon Nan kissed me and Milly, and then kissed Mrs. Nelson. In that radiant moment Nan was all sweetness.

"It is the Rube's break into fast company," she said.

The Knocker

YES, Carroll, I got my notice. Maybe it's no surprise to you. And there's one more thing I want to say. You're 'it' on this team. You're the topnotch catcher in the Western League and one of the best ball players in the game—but you're a knocker!"

Madge Ellston heard young Sheldon speak. She saw the flash in his gray eyes and the heat of his bronzed face as he looked intently at the big catcher.

"Fade away, sonny. Back to the bush-league for yours!" replied Carroll, derisively. "You're not fast enough for Kansas City. You look pretty good in a uniform and you're swift on your feet, but you can't hit. You've got a glass arm and you run bases like an ostrich trying to side. That notice was coming to you. Go learn the game!"

Then a crowd of players trooped noisily out of the hotel lobby and swept Sheldon and Carroll down the porch steps toward the waiting omnibus.

Madge's uncle owned the Kansas City club. She had lived most of her nineteen years in a baseball atmosphere, but accustomed as she was to baseball talk and the peculiar banterings and bickerings of the players, there were times when it seemed all Greek. If a player got his "notice" it meant he would be released in ten days. A "knocker" was a ball player who spoke ill of his fellow players. This scrap of conversation, however, had an unusual interest because Carroll had paid court to her for a year, and Sheldon, coming to the team that spring, had fallen desperately in love with her. She liked Sheldon pretty well, but Carroll fascinated her. She began to wonder if there were bad feelings between the rivals—to compare them—to get away from herself and judge them impersonally.

When Pat Donahue, the veteran manager of the team came out, Madge greeted him with a smile. She had always gotten on famously with Pat, notwithstanding her imperious desire to handle the managerial reins herself upon occasions. Pat beamed all over his round ruddy face.

"Miss Madge, you weren't to the park yesterday an' we lost without our pretty mascot. We shure needed you. Denver's playin' at a fast clip."

"I'm coming out today," replied Miss Ellston, thoughtfully. "Pat, what's a knocker?"

"Now, Miss Madge, are you askin' me that after I've been coachin' you in baseball for years?" questioned Pat, in distress.

"I know what a knocker is, as everybody else does. But I want to know the real meaning, the inside-ball of it, to use your favorite saying."

Studying her grave face with shrewd eyes Donahue slowly lost his smile.

"The inside-ball of it, eh? Come, let's sit over here a bit—the sun's shure warm today. . . . Miss Madge, a knocker is the strangest man known in the game, the hardest to deal with an' what every baseball manager hates most."

Donahue told her that he believed the term "knocker" came originally from baseball; that in general it typified the player who strengthened his own standing by belittling the ability of his teammates, and by enlarging upon his own superior qualities. But there were many phases of this peculiar type. Some players were natural born knockers; others acquired the name in their later years in the game when younger men threatened to win their places. Some of the best players ever produced by baseball had the habit in its most violent form. There were players of ridiculously poor ability who held their jobs on the strength of this one trait. It was a mystery how they misled magnates and managers alike; how for months they held their places, weakening a team, often keeping a good team down in the race; all from sheer bold suggestion of their own worth and other players' worthlessness. Strangest of all was the knockers' power to disorganize; to engender a bad spirit between management and team and among the players. The team which was without one of the parasites of the game generally stood well up in the race for the pennant, though there had been championship teams noted for great knockers as well as great players.

"It's shure strange, Miss Madge," said Pat in conclusion, shaking his gray head. "I've played hundreds of knockers, an' released them, too. Knockers always get it in the end, but they go on foolin' me and workin' me just the same as if I was a youngster with my first team. They're part an' parcel of the game."

"Do you like these men off the field—outside of baseball, I mean?"

"No, I shure don't, an' I never seen one yet that wasn't the same off the field as he was on."

"Thank you, Pat. I think I understand now. And—oh, yes, there's another thing I want to ask you. What's the matter with Billie Sheldon? Uncle George said he was falling off in his game. Then I've read the papers. Billie started out well in the spring."

"Didn't he? I was sure thinkin' I had a find in Billie. Well, he's lost his nerve. He's in a bad slump. It's worried me for days. I'm goin' to release Billie. The team needs a shake-up. That's where Billie gets the worst of it, for he's really the makin' of a star; but he's slumped, an' now knockin' has made him let down. There, Miss Madge, that's an example of what I've just been tellin' you. An' you can see that a manager has his troubles. These hulkin' athletes are a lot of spoiled babies an' I often get sick of my job."

That afternoon Miss Ellston was in a brown study all the way out to the baseball park. She arrived rather earlier than usual to find the grandstand empty. The Denver team had just come upon the field, and the Kansas City players were practising batting at the left of the diamond. Madge walked down the aisle of the grandstand and out along the reporters' boxes. She asked one of the youngsters on the field to tell Mr. Sheldon that she would like to speak with him a moment.

Billie eagerly hurried from the players' bench with a look of surprise and expectancy on his suntanned face. Madge experienced for the first time a sudden sense of shyness at his coming. His lithe form and his nimble step somehow gave her a pleasure that seemed old yet was new. When he neared her, and, lifting his cap, spoke her name, the shade of gloom in his eyes and lines of trouble on his face dispelled her confusion.

"Billie, Pat tells me he's given you ten days' notice," she said.

"It's true."

"What's wrong with you, Billie?"

"Oh, I've struck a bad streak—can't hit or throw."

"Are you a quitter?"

"No, I'm not," he answered quickly, flushing a dark red.

"You started off this spring with a rush. You played

brilliantly and for a while led the team in batting. Uncle George thought so well of you. Then came this spell of bad form. But, Billie, it's only a slump; you can brace.''

"I don't know,'' he replied, despondently. "Awhile back I got my mind off the game. Then—people who don't like me have taken advantage of my slump to—''

"To knock,'' interrupted Miss Ellston.

"I'm not saying that,'' he said, looking away from her.

"But I'm saying it. See here, Billie Sheldon, my uncle owns this team and Pat Donahue is manager. I think they both like me a little. Now I don't want to see you lose your place. Perhaps—''

"Madge, that's fine of you—but I think—I guess it'd be best for me to leave Kansas City.''

"Why?''

"You know,'' he said huskily. "I've lost my head— I'm in love—I can't think of baseball—I'm crazy about you.''

Miss Ellston's sweet face grew rosy, clear to the tips of her ears.

"Billie Sheldon,'' she replied, spiritedly. "You're talking nonsense. Even if you were—were that way, it'd be no reason to play poor ball. Don't throw the game, as Pat would say. Make a brace! Get up on your toes! Don't quit!''

She exhausted her vocabulary of baseball language if not her enthusiasm, and paused in blushing confusion.

"Madge!''

"Will you brace up?''

"Will I—will I!'' he exclaimed, breathlessly.

Madge murmured a hurried good-bye and, turning away, went up the stairs. Her uncle's private box was upon the top of the grandstand and she reached it in a somewhat bewildered state of mind. She had a confused sense of having appeared to encourage Billie, and did not know whether she felt happy or guilty. The flame in his eyes had warmed all her blood. Then, as she glanced over the railing to see the powerful Burns Carroll, there rose in her breast a panic at strange variance with her other feelings.

Many times had Madge Ellston viewed the field and stands and the outlying country from this high vantage point; but never with the same mingling emotions, nor had the sunshine ever been so golden, the woods and meadows so green, the diamond so smooth and velvety, the whole scene so gaily bright.

Denver had always been a good drawing card, and having won the first game of the present series, bade fair to draw a record attendance. The long lines of bleachers, already packed with the familiar mottled crowd, sent forth a merry, rattling hum. Soon a steady stream of well-dressed men and women poured in the gates and up the grandstand stairs. The soft murmur of many voices in light conversation and laughter filled the air. The peanut venders and scorecard sellers kept up their insistent shrill cries. The baseball park was alive now and restless; the atmosphere seemed charged with freedom and pleasure. The players romped like skittish colts, the fans shrieked their witticisms—all sound and movements suggested play.

Madge Ellston was somehow relieved to see her uncle sitting in one of the lower boxes. During this game she wanted to be alone, and she believed she would be, for the president of the League and directors of the Kansas City team were with her uncle. When the bell rang to call the Denver team in from practice the stands could hold no more, and the roped-off sidelines were filling up with noisy men and boys. From her seat Madge could see right down upon the players' bench, and when she caught both Sheldon and Carroll gazing upward she drew back with sharply contrasted thrills.

Then the bell rang again, the bleachers rolled out their welcoming acclaim, and play was called with Kansas City at the bat.

Right off the reel Hunt hit a short fly safely over second. The ten thousand spectators burst into a roar. A good start liberated applause and marked the feeling for the day.

Madge was surprised and glad to see Billie Sheldon start next for the plate. All season, until lately, he had been the second batter. During his slump he had been relegated to the last place on the batting list. Perhaps he had asked Pat to try him once more at the top. The bleachers voiced their unstinted appreciation of this return, showing that Billie still had a strong hold on their hearts.

As for Madge, her breast heaved and she had difficulty in breathing. This was going to be a hard game for her. The intensity of her desire to see Billie brace up to his old form amazed her. And Carroll's rude words beat thick in her ears. Never before had Billie appeared so instinct with life, so intent and strung as when he faced Keene, the Denver pitcher. That worthy tied himself up in a knot, and then, unlimbering a long arm, delivered the brand new ball.

Billie seemed to leap forward and throw his bat at it. There was a sharp ringing crack—and the ball was like a white string marvelously stretching out over the players, over the green field beyond, and then, sailing, soaring, over the right-field fence. For a moment the stands, even the bleachers, were stone quiet. No player had ever hit a ball over that fence. It had been deemed impossible, as was attested to by the many painted "ads" offering prizes for such a feat. Suddenly the far end of the bleachers exploded and the swelling roar rolled up to engulf the grandstand in thunder. Billie ran round the bases to applause never before vented on that field. But he gave no sign that it affected him; he did not even doff his cap. White-faced and stern, he hurried to the bench, where Pat fell all over him and many of the players grasped his hands.

Up in her box Madge was crushing her scorecard and whispering: "Oh! Billie, I could hug you for that!"

Two runs on two pitched balls! That was an opening to stir an exacting audience to the highest pitch of enthusiasm. The Denver manager peremptorily called Keene off the diamond and sent in Steele, a southpaw, who had always bothered Pat's left-handed hitters. That move showed his astute judgment, for Steele struck out McReady and retired Curtis and Mahew on easy chances.

It was Dalgren's turn to pitch and though he had shown promise in several games he had not yet been tried out on a team of Denver's strength. The bleachers gave him a good cheering as he walked into the box, but for all that they whistled their wonder at Pat's assurance in putting him against the Cowboys in an important game.

The lad was visibly nervous and the hard-hitting and loud-coaching Denver players went after him as if they meant to drive him out of the game. Crane stung one to left center for a base, Moody was out on a liner to short, almost doubling up Crane; the fleet-footed Bluett bunted and beat the throw to first; Langly drove to left for what seemed a three-bagger, but Curtis, after a hard run, caught the ball almost off the left-field bleachers. Crane and Bluett advanced a base on the throw-in. Then Kane batted up a high foul-fly. Burns Carroll, the Kansas City catcher, had the reputation of being a fiend for chasing foul flies, and he dashed at this one with a speed that threatened a hard fall over the players' bench or a collision with the fence. Carroll caught the ball and crashed against the grandstand, but leaped back with an agility that showed that if there was any harm done it had not been to him.

Thus the sharp inning ended with a magnificent play. It electrified the spectators into a fierce energy of applause. With one accord, by baseball instinct, the stands and bleachers and roped-in-sidelines realized it was to be a game of games and they answered to the stimulus with a savage enthusiasm that inspired ballplayers to great plays.

In the first half of the second inning, Steele's will to do and his arm to execute were very like his name. Kansas City could not score. In their half the Denver team made one run by clean hitting.

Then the closely fought advantage seesawed from one team to the other. It was not a pitchers' battle, though both men worked to the limit of skill and endurance. They were hit hard. Dazzling plays kept the score down and the innings short. Over the fields hung the portent of something to come, every player, every spectator felt the subtle baseball chance; each inning seemed to lead closer and more thrillingly up to the climax. But at the end of the seventh, with the score tied six and six, with daring steals, hard hits, and splendid plays, enough to have made memorable several games, it seemed that the great portentous moment was still in abeyance.

The head of the batting list for Kansas City was up. Hunt caught the first pitched ball squarely on the end of his bat. It was a mighty drive; and as the ball soared and soared over the centerfield, Hunt raced down the base line, and the winged-footed Crane sped outward, the bleachers split their throats. The hit looked good for a home run, but Crane leaped up and caught the ball in his gloved hand. The sudden silence and then the long groan which racked the bleachers was greater tribute to Crane's play than any applause.

Billie Sheldon then faced Steele. The fans roared hoarsely, for Billie had hit safely three times out of four. Steele used his curve ball, but he could not get the batter to go after it. When he had wasted three balls, the never-despairing bleachers howled: "Now, Billie, in your groove! Sting the next one!" But Billie waited. One strike! Two strikes! Steele cut the plate. That was a test which proved Sheldon's caliber.

With seven innings of exciting play passed, with both teams on edge, with the bleachers wild and the grandstands keyed up to the breaking point, with everything making deliberation almost impossible, Billie Sheldon had remorselessly waited for three balls and two strikes.

"Now! . . . Now! . . . Now!" shrieked the bleachers.

Steele had not tired nor lost his cunning. With hands before him he grimly studied Billie, then whirling hard to get more weight into his motion, he threw the ball.

Billie swung perfectly and cut a curving liner between the first baseman and the base. Like a shot it skipped over the grass out along the foul line into right field. Amid tremendous uproar Billie stretched the hit into a triple, and when he got up out of the dust after his slide into third the noise seemed to be the crashing down of the bleachers. It died out with the choking gurgling yell of the most leather-lunged fan.

"O-o-o-o-you-Billie-e!"

McReady marched up and promptly hit a long fly to the redoubtable Crane. Billie crouched in a sprinter's position with his eye on the graceful fielder, waiting confidently for the ball to drop. As if there had not already been sufficient heart-rending moments, the chance that governed baseball meted out this play; one of the keenest, most trying known to the game. Players waited, spectators waited, and the instant of that dropping ball was interminably long. Everybody knew Crane would catch it; everybody thought of the wonderful throwing arm that had made him famous. Was it possible for Billie Sheldon to beat the throw to the plate?

Crane made the catch and got the ball away at the same instant Sheldon leaped from the base and dashed for home. Then all eyes were on the ball. It seemed incredible that a ball thrown by human strength could speed plateward so low, so straight, so swift. But it lost its force and slanted down to bound into the catcher's hands just as Billie slid over the plate.

By the time the bleachers had stopped stamping and bawling, Curtis ended the inning with a difficult grounder to the infield.

Once more the Kansas City players took the field and Burns Carroll sang out in his lusty voice: "Keep lively, boys! Play hard! Dig 'em up an' get 'em!" Indeed the big catcher was the mainstay of the home team. The bulk of the work fell upon his shoulders. Dalgren was wild and kept his catcher continually blocking low pitches and wide curves and poorly controlled high fast balls. But they were all alike to Carroll. Despite his weight, he was as nimble on his feet as a goat, and if he once got his hands on the ball he never missed it. It was his encouragement that steadied Dalgren; his judgment of hitters that carried the young pitcher through dangerous places; his lightning swift grasp of points that directed the machine-like work of his team.

In this inning Carroll exhibited another of his demon chases after a foul fly; he threw the base-stealing Crane out at second, and by a remarkable leap and stop of Mc-Ready's throw, he blocked a runner who would have tied the score.

The Cowboys blanked their opponents in the first half of the ninth, and trotted in for their turn needing one run to tie, two runs to win.

There had scarcely been a breathing spell for the on-lookers in this rapid-fire game. Every inning had held them, one moment breathless, the next wildly clamorous, and another waiting in numb fear. What did these last few moments hold in store? The only answer to that was the dogged plugging optimism of the Denver players. To listen to them, to watch them, was to gather the impression that baseball fortune always favored them in the end.

"Only three more, Dal. Steady boys, it's our game," rolled out Carroll's deep bass. How virile he was! What a tower of strength to the weakening pitcher!

But valiantly as Dalgren tried to respond, he failed. The grind—the strain had been too severe. When he finally did locate the plate Bluett hit safely. Langley bunted along the base line and beat the ball.

A blank, dead quiet settled down over the bleachers and stands. Something fearful threatened. What might not come to pass, even at the last moment of this nerve-racking game? There was a runner on first and a runner on second. That was bad. Exceedingly bad was it that these runners were on base with nobody out. Worst of all was the fact that Kane was up. Kane, the best bunter, the fastest man to first, the hardest hitter in the league! That he would fail to advance those two runners was scarcely worth consideration. Once advanced, a fly to the outfield, a scratch, anything almost, would tie the score. So this was the climax presaged so many times earlier in the game. Dalgren seemed to wilt under it.

Kane swung his ash viciously and called on Dalgren to put one over. Dalgren looked in toward the bench as if he wanted and expected to be taken out. But Pat Donahue made no sign. Pat had trained many a pitcher by forcing him to take his medicine. Then Carroll, mask under his arm, rolling his big hand in his mitt, sauntered down to the pitcher's box. The sharp order of the umpire in no wise disconcerted him. He said something to Dalgren, vehemently nodding his head the while. Players and audience alike supposed he was trying to put a little heart into Dalgren, and liked him the better, notwithstanding the opposition to the umpire.

Carroll sauntered back to his position. He adjusted his breast protector, and put on his mask, deliberately taking his time. Then he stepped behind the plate, and after signing for the pitch, he slowly moved his right hand up to his mask.

Dalgren wound up, took his swing, and let drive. Even as he delivered the ball Carroll bounded away from his position, flinging off the mask as he jumped. For a single fleeting instant, the catcher's position was vacated. But that instant was long enough to make the audience gasp. Kane bunted beautifully down the third base line, and there Carroll stood, fifteen feet from the plate, agile as a huge monkey. He whipped the ball to Mahew at third. Mahew wheeled quick as thought and lined the ball to second. Sheldon came tearing for the bag, caught the ball on the run, and with a violent stop and wrench threw it like a bullet to first base. Fast as Kane was, the ball beat him ten feet. A triple play!

The players of both teams cheered, but the audience, slower to grasp the complex and intricate points, needed a long moment to realize what had happened. They needed another to divine that Carroll had anticipated Kane's intention to bunt, had left his position as the ball was pitched, had planned all, risked all, played all on Kane's sure eye; and so he had retired the side and won the game by creating and executing the rarest play in baseball.

Then the audience rose in a body to greet the great catcher. What a hoarse thundering roar shook the stands and waved in a blast over the field! Carroll stood bowing his acknowledgment, and then swaggered a little with the sun shining on his handsome heated face. Like a conqueror conscious of full blown power he stalked away to the clubhouse.

Madge Ellston came out of her trance and viewed the ragged scorecard, her torn parasol, her battered gloves and flying hair, her generally disheveled state with a little start of dismay, but when she got into the thick and press of the moving crowd she found all the women more or less disheveled. And they seemed all the prettier and friendlier for that. It was a happy crowd and voices were conspicuously hoarse.

When Madge entered the hotel parlor that evening she found her uncle with guests and among them was Burns Carroll. The presence of the handsome giant affected Madge more impellingly than ever before, yet in some inexplicably different way. She found herself trembling; she sensed a crisis in her feelings for this man and it frightened her. She became conscious suddenly that she had always been afraid of him. Watching Carroll receive the congratulations of many of those present, she saw that he dominated them as he had her. His magnetism was overpowering; his great stature seemed to fill the room; his easy careless assurance emanated from superior strength. When he spoke lightly of the game, of Crane's marvelous catch, of Dalgren's pitching, and of his own triple play, it seemed these looming features retreated in perspective—somehow lost their vital significance because he slighted them.

In the light of Carroll's illuminating talk, in the remembrance of Sheldon's bitter denunciation, in the knowledge of Pat Donahue's estimate of a peculiar type of ball player, Madge Ellston found herself judging the man —bravely trying to resist his charm, to be fair to him and to herself.

Carroll soon made his way to her side and greeted her with his old familiar manner of possession. However irritating it might be to Madge when alone, now it held her bound.

Carroll possessed the elemental attributes of a conqueror. When with him Madge whimsically feared that he would snatch her up in his arms and carry her bodily off, as the warriors of old did with the women they wanted.

But she began to believe that the fascination he exercised upon her was merely physical. That gave her pause. Not only was Burns Carroll on trial, but also a very foolish fluttering little moth—herself. It was time enough, however, to be stern with herself after she had tried him.

"Wasn't that a splendid catch of Crane's today?" she asked.

"A lucky stab! Crane has a habit of running round like an ostrich and sticking out a hand to catch a ball. It's a grandstand play. Why, a good outfielder would have been waiting under that fly."

"Dalgren did fine work in the box, don't you think?"

"Oh, the kid's all right with an old head back of the plate. He's wild, though, and will never make good in fast company. I won his game today. He wouldn't have lasted an inning without me. It was dead wrong for Pat to pitch him. Dalgren simply can't pitch and he hasn't sand enough to learn."

A hot retort trembled upon Madge Ellston's lips, but she withheld it and quietly watched Carroll. How complacent he was, how utterly self-contained!

"And Billie Sheldon—wasn't it good to see him brace? What hitting! That home run!"

"Sheldon flashed up today. That's the worst of such players. This talk of his slump is all rot. When he joined the team he made some lucky hits and the papers lauded him as a comer, but he soon got down to his real form. Why, to break into a game now and then, to shut his eyes and hit a couple on the nose—that's not baseball. Pat's given him ten days' notice, and his release will be a good move for the team. Sheldon's not fast enough for this league."

"I'm sorry. He seemed so promising," replied Madge. "I liked Billy—pretty well."

"Yes, that was evident," said Carroll, firing up. "I

never could understand what you saw in him. Why, Sheldon's no good. He—"

Madge turned a white face that silenced Carroll. She excused herself and returned to the parlor, where she had last seen her uncle. Not finding him there, she went into the long corridor and met Sheldon, Dalgren, and two more of the players. Madge congratulated the young pitcher and the other players on their brilliant work; and they, not to be outdone, gallantly attributed the day's victory to her presence at the game. Then, without knowing in the least how it came about, she presently found herself alone with Billy, and they were strolling into the music room.

"Madge, did I brace up?"

The girl risked one quick look at him. How boyish he seemed, how eager! What an altogether different Billie! But was the difference all in him! Somehow, despite a conscious shyness in the moment she felt natural and free, without the uncertainty and restraint that had always troubled her while with him.

"Oh, Billie, that glorious home run!"

"Madge, wasn't that hit a dandy? How I made it is a mystery, but the bat felt like a feather. I thought of you. Tell me—what did you think when I hit that ball over the fence?"

"Billie, I'll never, never tell you."

"Yes—please—I want to know. Didn't you think something—nice of me?"

The pink spots in Madge's cheeks widened to crimson flames.

"Billie, are you still—crazy about me? Now, don't come so close. Can't you behave yourself? And don't break my fingers with your terrible baseball hands. . . . Well, when you made that hit I just collapsed and I said—"

"Say it! Say it!" implored Billie.

She lowered her face and then bravely raised it.

"I said, 'Billie, I could hug you for that!' . . . Billie, let me go! Oh, you mustn't!—please!"

Quite a little while afterward Madge remembered to tell Billie that she had been seeking her uncle. They met him and Pat Donahue, coming out of the parlor.

"Where have you been all evening?" demanded Mr. Ellston.

"Shure it looks as if she's signed a new manager," said Pat, his shrewd eyes twinkling.

The soft glow in Madge's cheeks deepened into tell-tale scarlet; Billie resembled a schoolboy stricken in guilt.

"Aha! so that's it?" queried her uncle.

"Ellston," said Pat. "Billie's home-run drive today recalled his notice an' if I don't miss guess it won him another game—the best game in life."

"By George!" exclaimed Mr. Ellston. "I was afraid it was Carroll!"

He led Madge away and Pat followed with Billie.

"Shure, it was good to see you brace, Billie," said the manager, with a kindly hand on the young man's arm. "I'm tickled to death. That ten days' notice doesn't go. See? I've had to shake up the team but your job is good. I released McReady outright an' traded Carroll to Denver for a catcher and a fielder. Some of the directors hollered murder, an' I expect the fans will roar, but I'm running this team, I'll have harmony among my players. Carroll is a great catcher, but he's a knocker."

The Winning Ball

ONE day in July our Rochester club, leader in the Eastern League, had returned to the hotel after winning a double-header from the Syracuse club. For some occult reason there was to be a lay-off next day and then on the following another double-header. These double-headers we hated next to exhibition games. Still a lay-off for twenty-four hours, at that stage of the race, was a Godsend, and we received the news with exclamations of pleasure.

After dinner we were all sitting and smoking comfortably in front of the hotel when our manager, Merritt, came hurriedly out of the lobby. It struck me that he appeared a little flustered.

"Say, you fellars," he said brusquely. "Pack your suits and be ready for the bus at seven-thirty."

For a moment there was a blank, ominous silence, while we assimilated the meaning of his terse speech.

"I've got a good thing on for tomorrow," continued the manager. "Sixty-per-cent gate receipts if we win. That Guelph team is hot stuff, though."

"Guelph!" exclaimed some of the players suspiciously. "Where's Guelph?"

"It's in Canada. We'll take the night express an' get there tomorrow in time for the game. An' we'll hev to hustle."

Upon Merritt then rained a multiplicity of excuses. Gillinger was not well, and ought to have that day's rest. Snead's eyes would profit by a lay-off. Deerfoot Browning was leading the league in base running, and as his legs were all bruised and scraped by sliding, a manager who was not an idiot would have a care of such valuable runmakers for his team. Lake had "Charley-horse." Hathaway's arm was sore. Bane's stomach threatened gastritis. Spike Doran's finger needed a chance to heal. I was stale, and the other players, three pitchers, swore their arms should be in the hospital.

"Cut it out!" said Merritt, getting exasperated. "You'd all lay down on me—now, wouldn't you? Well, listen to this: McDougal pitched today; he doesn't go. Blake works Friday, he doesn't go. But the rest of you puffed-up, high-salaried stiffs pack your grips quick. See? It'll cost any fresh fellar fifty for missin' the train."

So that was how eleven of the Rochester team found themselves moodily boarding a Pullman *en route* for Buffalo and Canada. We went to bed early and arose late.

Guelph lay somewhere in the interior of Canada, and we did not expect to get there until 1 o'clock.

As it turned out, the train was late; we had to dress hurriedly in the smoking room, pack our citizen clothes in our grips, and leave the train to go direct to the ball grounds without time for lunch.

It was a tired, dusty-eyed, peevish crowd of ball players that climbed into a waiting bus at the little station.

We had never heard of Guelph; we did not care anything about Rube baseball teams. Baseball was not play to us; it was the hardest kind of work, and of all things an exhibition game was an abomination.

The Guelph players, strapping lads, met us with every

mark of respect and courtesy and escorted us to the field with a brass band that was loud in welcome, if not harmonious in tune.

Some 500 men and boys trotted curiously along with us, for all the world as if the bus were a circus parade cage filled with striped tigers. What a rustic, motley crowd massed about in and on that ball ground. There must have been 10,000.

The audience was strange to us. The Indians, half-breeds, French-Canadians; the huge, hulking, bearded farmers or traders, or trappers, whatever they were, were new to our baseball experience.

The players themselves, however, earned the largest share of our attention. By the time they had practiced a few moments we looked at Merritt and Merritt looked at us.

These long, powerful, big-handed lads evidently did not know the difference between lacrosse and baseball; but they were quick as cats on their feet, and they scooped up the ball in a way wonderful to see. And throw!—it made a professional's heart swell just to see them line the ball across the diamond.

"Lord! What whips these lads have!" exclaimed Merritt. "Hope we're not up against it. If this team should beat us we wouldn't draw a handful at Toronto. We can't afford to be beaten. Jump around and cinch the game quick. If we get in a bad place, I'll sneak in the 'rabbit.' "

The "rabbit" was a baseball similar in appearance to the ordinary league ball: under its horsehide cover, however, it was remarkably different.

An ingenious fan, a friend of Merritt, had removed the covers from a number of league balls and sewed them on rubber balls of his own making. They could not be distinguished from the regular article, not even by an experienced professional—until they were hit. Then! The fact that after every bounce one of these rubber balls bounded swifter and higher had given it the name of the "rabbit."

Many a game had the "rabbit" won for us at critical stages. Of course it was against the rules of the league, and of course every player in the league knew about it; still, when it was judiciously and cleverly brought into a close game, the "rabbit" would be in play, and very probably over the fence, before the opposing captain could learn of it, let alone appeal to the umpire.

"Fellars, look at that guy who's goin' to pitch," suddenly spoke up one of the team.

Many as were the country players whom we seasoned and traveled professionals had run across, this twirler outclassed them for remarkable appearance. Moreover, what put an entirely different tinge to our momentary humor was the discovery that he was as wild as a March hare and could throw a ball so fast that it resembled a pea shot from a boy's air gun.

Deerfoot led our batting list, and after the first pitched ball, which he did not see, and the second, which ticked his shirt as it shot past, he turned to us with an expression that made us groan inwardly.

When Deerfoot looked that way it meant the pitcher was dangerous. Deerfoot made no effort to swing at the next ball, and was promptly called out on strikes.

I was second at bat, and went up with some reluctance. I happened to be leading the league in both long distance and safe hitting, and I doted on speed. But having stopped many mean inshoots with various parts of my anatomy, I was rather squeamish about facing backwoods yaps who had no control.

When I had watched a couple of his pitches, which the umpire called strikes, I gave him credit for as much speed as Rusie. These balls were as straight as a string, singularly without curve, jump, or variation of any kind. I lined the next one so hard at the shortstop that it cracked like a pistol as it struck his hands and whirled him half off his feet. Still he hung to the ball and gave opportunity for the first crash of applause.

"Boys, he's a trifle wild," I said to my teammates, "but he has the most beautiful ball to hit you ever saw. I don't believe he uses a curve, and when we once time that speed we'll kill it."

Next inning, after old man Hathaway had baffled the Canadians with his wide, tantalizing curves, my predictions began to be verified. Snead rapped one high and far to deep right field. To our infinite surprise, however, the right fielder ran with fleetness that made our own Deerfoot seem slow, and he got under the ball and caught it.

Doran sent a sizzling grasscutter down toward left. The lanky third baseman darted over, dived down, and, coming up with the ball, exhibited the power of a throwing arm that made us all green with envy.

Then, when the catcher chased a foul fly somewhere back in the crowd and caught it, we began to take notice.

"Lucky stabs!" said Merritt cheerfully. "They can't keep that up. We'll drive him to the woods next time."

But they did keep it up; moreover, they became more brilliant as the game progressed. What with Hathaway's heady pitching we soon disposed of them when at the bat; our turns, however, owing to the wonderful fielding of these backwoodsmen, were also fruitless.

Merritt, with his mind ever on the slice of gate money coming if we won, began to fidget and fume and find fault.

"You're a swell lot of champions, now, ain't you?" he observed between innings.

All baseball players like to bat, and nothing pleases them so much as base hits; on the other hand, nothing is quite so painful as to send out hard liners only to see them caught. And it seemed as if every man on our team connected with that lanky twirler's fast high ball and hit with the force that made the bat spring only to have one of these rubes get his big hands upon it.

Considering that we were in no angelic frame of mind before the game started, and in view of Merritt's persistently increasing ill humor, this failure of ours to hit a ball safely gradually worked us into a kind of frenzy. From indifference we passed to determination, and from that to sheer passionate purpose.

Luck appeared to be turning in the sixth inning. With one out, Lake hit a beauty to right. Doran beat an infield grounder and reached first. Hathaway struck out.

With Browning up and me next, the situation looked rather precarious for the Canadians.

"Say, Deerfoot," whispered Merritt, "dump one down the third-base line. He's playin' deep. It's a pipe. Then the bases will be full an' Reddy'll clean up."

In a stage like that Browning was a man absolutely to depend upon. He placed a slow bunt in the grass toward third and sprinted for first. The third baseman fielded the ball, but, being confused, did not know where to throw it.

"Stick it in your basket," yelled Merritt, in a delight that showed how hard he was pulling for the gate money, and his beaming smile as he turned to me was inspiring. "Now, Reddy, it's up to you! I'm not worrying about what's happened so far. I know, with you at bat in a pinch, it's all off!"

Merritt's compliment was pleasing, but it did not augment my purpose, for that already had reached the highest mark. Love of hitting, if no other thing, gave me the thrilling fire to arise to the opportunity. Selecting my light bat, I went up and faced the rustic twirler and softly said things to him.

He delivered the ball, and I could have yelled aloud, so fast, so straight, so true it sped toward me. Then I hit it harder than I had ever hit a ball in my life. The bat sprung, as if it were whalebone. And the ball took a bullet course between center and left. So beautiful a hit was it that I watched as I ran.

Out of the tail of my eye I saw the center fielder running. When I rounded first base I got a good look at this fielder, and though I had seen the greatest outfielders the game ever produced, I never saw one that covered ground so swiftly as he.

On the ball soared, and began to drop; on the fielder sped, and began to disappear over a little hill back of his position. Then he reached up with a long arm and marvelously caught the ball in one hand. He went out of sight as I touched second base, and the heterogeneous crowd knew about a great play to make more noise than a herd of charging buffalo.

In the next half inning our opponents, by clean drives, scored two runs and we in our turn again went out ignominiously. When the first of the eighth came we were desperate and clamored for the "rabbit."

"I've sneaked it in," said Merritt, with a low voice. "Got it to the umpire on the last passed ball. See, the pitcher's got it now. Boys, it's all off but the fireworks! Now, break loose!"

A peculiarity about the "rabbit" was the fact that though it felt as light as the regulation league ball it could not be thrown with the same speed and to curve it was an impossibility.

Bane hit the first delivery from our hoosier stumbling block. The ball struck the ground and began to bound toward short. With every bound it went swifter, longer and higher, and it bounced clear over the shortstop's head. Lake chopped one in front of the plate, and it rebounded from the ground straight up so high that both runners were safe before it came down.

Doran hit to the pitcher. The ball caromed his leg, scooted fiendishly at the second baseman, and tried to run up all over him like a tame squirrel. Bases full!

Hathaway got a safe fly over the infield and two runs tallied. The pitcher, in spite of the help of the umpire, could not locate the plate for Balknap, and gave him a base on balls. Bases full again!

Deerfoot slammed a hot liner straight at the second baseman, which, striking squarely in his hands, recoiled as sharply as if it had struck a wall. Doran scored, and still the bases were filled.

The laboring pitcher began to get rattled; he could not find his usual speed; he knew it, but evidently could not account for it.

When I came to bat, indications were not wanting that the Canadian team would soon be up in the air. The long pitcher delivered the "rabbit," and got it low down by my knees, which was an unfortunate thing for him. I swung on that one, and trotted round the bases behind the runners while the center and left fielders chased the ball.

Gillinger weighed nearly two hundred pounds, and he got all his weight under the "rabbit." It went so high that we could scarcely see it. All the infielders rushed in, and after staggering around, with heads bent back, one of them, the shortstop, managed to get under it. The "rabbit" bounded forty feet out of his hands!

When Snead's grounder nearly tore the third baseman's leg off; when Bane's hit proved as elusive as a flitting shadow; when Lake's liner knocked the pitcher flat, and Doran's fly leaped high out of the center fielder's glove—then those earnest, simple, country ballplayers realized something was wrong. But they imagined it was in themselves, and after a short spell of rattles, they steadied up and tried harder than ever. The motions they went through trying to stop that jumping jackrabbit of a ball were ludicrous in the extreme.

Finally, through a foul, a short fly, and a scratch hit

to first, they retired the side and we went into the field with the score 14 to 2 in our favor.

But Merritt had not found it possible to get the "rabbit" out of play!

We spent a fatefully anxious few moments squabbling with the umpire and captain over the "rabbit." At the idea of letting those herculean railsplitters have a chance to hit the rubber ball we felt our blood run cold.

"But this ball has a rip in it," blustered Gillinger. He lied atrociously. A microscope could not have discovered as much as a scratch in that smooth leather.

"Sure it has," supplemented Merritt, in the suave tones of a stage villain. "We're used to playin' with good balls."

"Why did you ring this one in on us?" asked the captain. "We never threw out this ball. We want a chance to hit it."

That was just the one thing we did not want them to have. But fate played against us.

"Get up on your toes, now an' dust," said Merritt. "Take your medicine, you lazy sit-in-front-of-the-hotel stiffs! Think of pay day!"

Not improbably we all entertained the identical thought that old man Hathaway was the last pitcher under the sun calculated to be effective with the "rabbit." He never relied on speed; in fact, Merritt often scornfully accused him of being unable to break a pane of glass; he used principally what we called floaters and a change of pace. Both styles were absolutely impractical with the "rabbit."

"It's comin' to us, all right, all right!" yelled Deerfoot to me, across the intervening grass. I was of the opinion that it did not take any genius to make Deerfoot's ominous prophecy.

Old man Hathaway gazed at Merritt on the bench as if he wished the manager could hear what he was calling him and then at his fellow-players as if both to warn and beseech them. Then he pitched the "rabbit."

Crack!

The big lumbering Canadian rapped the ball at Crab Bane. I did not see it, because it went so fast, but I gathered from Crab's actions that it must have been hit in his direction. At any rate, one of his legs flopped out sidewise as if it had been suddenly jerked, and he fell in a heap. The ball, a veritable "rabbit" in its wild jumps, headed on for Deerfoot, who contrived to stop it with his knees.

The next batter resembled the first one, and the hit likewise, only it leaped wickedly at Doran and went through his hands as if they had been paper. The third man batted up a very high fly to Gillinger. He clutched at it with his huge shovel hands, but he could not hold it. The way he pounced upon the ball, dug it out of the grass, and hurled it at Hathaway, showed his anger.

Obviously Hathaway had to stop the throw, for he could not get out of the road, and he spoke to his captain in what I knew were no complimentary terms.

Thus began retribution. Those husky lads continued to hammer the "rabbit" at the infielders, and as it bounced harder at every bounce so they batted harder at every bat.

Another singular feature about the "rabbit" was the seeming impossibility for professionals to hold it. Their familiarity with it, their understanding of its vagaries and inconsistencies, their mortal dread made fielding it a much more difficult thing than for their opponents.

By way of variety, the lambasting Canadians commenced to lambast a few over the hills and far away, which chased Deerfoot and me until our tongues lolled out.

Every time a run crossed the plate the motley crowd howled, roared, danced, and threw up their hats. The members of the batting team pranced up and down the sidelines, giving a splendid imitation of cannibals celebrating the occasion of a feast.

Once Snead stooped down to trap the "rabbit," and it slipped through his legs, for which his comrades jeered him unmercifully. Then a brawny batter sent up a tremendously high fly between short and third.

"You take it!" yelled Gillinger to Bane.

"You take it!" replied the Crab, and actually walked backward. That ball went a mile high. The sky was hazy, gray, the most perplexing in which to judge a fly ball. An ordinary fly gave trouble enough in the gauging.

Gillinger wandered around under the ball for what seemed an age. It dropped as swiftly as a rocket shoots upward. Gillinger went forward in a circle, then side-stepped, and threw up his broad hands. He misjudged the ball, and it hit him fairly on the head and bounced almost to where Doran stood at second.

Our big captain wilted. Time was called. But Gillinger, when he came to, refused to leave the game and went back to third with a lump on his head as large as a goose egg.

Every one of his teammates was sorry, yet every one howled in glee. To be hit on the head was the unpardonable sin for a professional.

Old man Hathaway gradually lost what little speed he had, and with it his nerve. Every time he pitched the "rabbit" he dodged. That was about the funniest and strangest thing ever seen on a ball field. Yet it had an element of tragedy.

Hathaway's expert contortions saved his head and body on divers occasions, but presently a low bounder glanced off the grass and manifested an affinity for his leg.

We all knew from the crack and the way the pitcher went down that the "rabbit" had put him out of the game. The umpire called time, and Merritt came running on the diamond.

"Hard luck, old man," said the manager. "That'll make a green and yellow spot all right. Boys, we're still two runs to the good. There's one out, an' we can win yet. Deerfoot, you're as badly crippled as Hathaway. The bench for yours. Hooker will go to center, an' I'll pitch."

Merritt's idea did not strike us as a bad one. He could pitch, and he always kept his arm in prime condition. We welcomed him into the fray for two reasons—because he might win the game, and because he might be overtaken by the baseball Nemesis.

While Merritt was putting on Hathaway's baseball shoes, some of us endeavored to get the "rabbit" away from the umpire, but he was too wise.

Merritt received the innocent-looking ball with a look of mingled disgust and fear, and he summarily ordered us to our positions.

Not far had we gone, however, when we were electrified by the umpire's sharp words: "Naw! Naw, you don't. I saw you change the ball I gave you fer one in your pocket! Naw! You don't come enny of your American dodges on us! Gimmee thet ball, an' you use the other, or I'll stop the game."

Wherewith the shrewd umpire took the ball from Merritt's hand and fished the "rabbit" from his pocket. Our thwarted manager stuttered his wrath. "Y-you be-be-wh-whiskered y-yap! I'll g-g-give—"

What dire threat he had in mind never materialized, for he became speechless. He glowered upon the cool little umpire, and then turned grandly toward the plate.

It may have been imagination, yet I made sure Merritt seemed to shrink and grow smaller before he pitched a ball. For one thing the plate was uphill from the pitcher's box, and then the fellow standing there loomed up like a hill and swung a bat that would have served as a wagon tongue. No wonder Merritt evinced nervousness. Presently he whirled and delivered the ball.

Bing!

A dark streak and a white puff of dust over second base showed how safe that hit was. By dint of manful body work, Hooker contrived to stop the "rabbit" in mid-center. Another run scored. Human nature was proof against this temptation, and Merritt's players tendered him manifold congratulations and dissertations.

"Grand, you old skinflint, grand!"

"There was a two-dollar bill stickin' on thet hit. Why didn't you stop it?"

"Say, Merritt, what little brains you've got will presently be ridin' on the 'rabbit.' "

"You will chase up these exhibition games!"

"Take your medicine now. Ha! Ha! Ha!"

After these merciless taunts, and particularly after the next slashing hit that tied the score, Merritt looked appreciably smaller and humbler.

He threw up another ball, and actually shied as it neared the plate.

The giant who was waiting to slug it evidently thought better of his eagerness as far as that pitch was concerned, for he let it go by.

Merritt got the next ball higher. With a mighty swing, the batsman hit a terrific liner right at the pitcher.

Quick as lightning, Merritt wheeled, and the ball struck him with the sound of two boards brought heavily together with a smack.

Merritt did not fall; he melted to the ground and writhed while the runners scored with more tallies than they needed to win.

What did we care? Justice had been done us, and we were unutterably happy. Crabe Bane stood on his head; Gillinger began a war dance; old man Hathaway hobbled out to the sidelines and whooped like an Indian; Snead rolled over and over in the grass. All of us broke out into typical expressions of baseball frenzy, and individual ones illustrating our particular moods.

Merritt got up and made a dive for the ball. With face positively flaming he flung it far beyond the merry crowd, over into a swamp. Then he limped for the bench. Which throw ended the most memorable game ever recorded to the credit of the "rabbit."

False Colors

F ATE has decreed more bad luck for Salisbury in Saturday's game with Bellville. It has leaked out that our rivals will come over strengthened by a 'ringer,' no less than Yale's star pitcher, Wayne. We saw him shut Princeton out in June, in the last game of the college year, and we are not optimistic in our predictions as to what Salisbury can do with him. This appears a rather unfair procedure for Bellville to resort to. Why couldn't they come over with their regular team? They have won a game, and so have we; both games were close and brilliant; the deciding game has roused unusual interest. We are inclined to resent Bellville's methods as unsportsmanlike. All our players can do is to go into this game on Saturday and try the harder to win."

Wayne laid down the Salisbury *Gazette*, with a little laugh of amusement, yet feeling a vague, disquieting sense of something akin to regret.

"Pretty decent of that chap not to roast me," he soliloquized.

Somewhere he had heard that Salisbury maintained an unsalaried team. It was notorious among college athletes that the Bellville Club paid for the services of distinguished players. And this in itself rather inclined Wayne to sympathize with Salisbury. He knew something of the struggles of a strictly amateur club to cope with its semi-professional rivals.

As he was sitting there, idly tipped back in a comfortable chair, dreaming over some of the baseball disasters he had survived before his college career, he saw a young man enter the lobby of the hotel, speak to the clerk, and then turn and come directly toward the window where Wayne was sitting.

"Are you Mr. Wayne, the Yale pitcher?" he asked eagerly. He was a fair-haired, clean-cut young fellow, and his voice rang pleasantly.

"Guilty," replied Wayne.

"My name's Huling. I'm captain of the Salisbury nine. Just learned you were in town and are going to pitch against us tomorrow. Won't you walk out into the grounds with me now? You might want to warm up a little."

"Thank you, yes, I will. Guess I won't need my suit. I'll just limber up, and give my arm a good rub."

It struck Wayne before they had walked far that Huling was an amiable and likable chap. As the captain of the Salisbury nine, he certainly had no reason to be agreeable to the Morristown "ringer," even though Wayne did happen to be a famous Yale pitcher.

The field was an oval, green as an emerald, level as a billiard table, and had no fences or stands to obstruct the open view of the surrounding wooded country. On each side of the diamond were rows of wooden benches, and at one end of the field stood a little clubhouse.

Wayne took off his coat, and tossed a ball for a while to an ambitious youngster, and then went into the clubhouse, where Huling introduced him to several of his players. After a good rubdown, Wayne thanked Huling for his courtesy, and started out, intending to go back to town.

"Why not stay to see us practice?" asked the captain. "We're not afraid you'll size up our weaknesses. As a matter of fact, we don't look forward to any hitting stunts tomorrow, eh, Burns? Burns, here, is our leading hitter, and he's been unusually noncommittal since he heard who was going to pitch for Bellville."

"Well, I wouldn't give a whole lot for my prospects of a home run tomorrow," said Burns, with a laugh.

Wayne went outside, and found a seat in the shade. A number of urchins had trooped upon the green field, and carriages and motors were already in evidence. By the time the players came out of the dressing room, ready for practice, there was quite a little crowd in attendance.

Despite Wayne's hesitation, Huling insisted upon introducing him to friends, and finally hauled him up to a big touring car full of girls. Wayne, being a Yale pitcher, had seen several thousand pretty girls, but the group in that automobile fairly dazzled him. And the last one to whom Huling presented him—with the words: "Dorothy, this is Mr. Wayne, the Yale pitcher, who is to play with Bellville tomorrow; Mr. Wayne, my sister"—was the girl he had known he would meet someday.

"Climb up, Mr. Wayne. We can make room," invited Miss Huling.

Wayne thought the awkwardness with which he found a seat beside her was unbecoming to a Yale senior. But, considering she was the girl he had been expecting to discover for years, his clumsiness bespoke the importance of the event. The merry laughter of the girls rang in his ears. Presently, a voice detached itself from the others, and came floating softly to him.

"Mr. Wayne, so you're going to wrest our laurels from us?" asked Miss Huling.

"I don't know—I'm not infallible—I've been beaten."

"When? Not this season?" she inquired quickly, be-traying a knowledge of his record that surprised and pleased him. "Mr. Wayne, I was at the Polo Grounds on June fifteenth."

Her white hand lightly touched the Princeton pin at her neck. Wayne roused suddenly out of his trance. The girl was a Princeton girl! The gleam of her golden hair, the flash of her blue eyes, became clear in sight.

"I'm very pleased to hear it," he replied.

"It was a great game, Mr. Wayne, and you may well be proud of your part in winning it. I shouldn't be sur-prised if you treated the Salisbury team to the same coat of whitewash. We girls are up in arms. Our boys stood a fair chance to win this game, but now there's a doubt. By the way, are you acquainted in Bellville?"

"No. I met Reed, the Bellville captain, in New York this week. He had already gotten an extra pitcher—an-other ringer—for this game, but he said he preferred me, if it could be arranged."

While conversing, Wayne made note of the fact that the other girls studiously left him to Miss Huling. If the avoidance had not been so marked, he would never have thought of it.

"Mr. Wayne, if your word is not involved—will you change your mind and pitch tomorrow's game for us in-stead of Bellville?"

Quite amazed, Wayne turned squarely to look at Miss Huling. Instead of disarming his quick suspicion, her cool, sweet voice, and brave, blue eyes confirmed it. The charms of the captain's sister were to be used to win him away from the Bellville nine. He knew the trick; it had been played upon him before.

But never had any other such occasion given him a feeling of regret. This case was different. She was the girl. And she meant to flirt with him, to use her eyes for all they were worth to encompass the Waterloo of the rival team.

No, he had made a mistake, after all—she was not the real girl. Suddenly conscious of a little shock of pain, he dismissed that dream girl from his mind, and determined to meet Miss Huling half way in her game. He could not flirt as well as he could pitch; still, he was no novice.

"Well, Miss Huling, my word certainly is not involved. But as to pitching for Salisbury—that depends."

"Upon what?"

"Upon what there is in it."

"Mr. Wayne, you mean—money? Oh, I know. My brother Rex told me how you college men are paid big sums. Our association will not give a dollar, and, besides, my brother knows nothing of this. But we girls are heart and soul on winning this game. We'll—"

"Miss Huling, I didn't mean remuneration in sordid cash," interrupted Wayne, in a tone that heightened the color in her cheeks.

Wayne eyed her keenly with mingled emotions. Was that rose-leaf flush in her cheeks natural? Some girls could blush at will. Were the wistful eyes, the earnest lips, only shamming? It cost him some bitterness to decide that they were. Her beauty fascinated, while it hardened him. Eternally, the beauty of women meant the undoing of men, whether they played the simple, inconsequential game of baseball, or the great, absorbing, mutable game of life.

The shame of the situation for him was increasingly annoying, inasmuch as this lovely girl should stoop to flirtation with a stranger, and the same time draw him, allure him, despite the apparent insincerity.

"Miss Huling, I'll pitch your game for two things," he continued.

"Name them."

"Wear Yale blue in place of that orange-and-black Princeton pin."

"I will." She said it with a shyness, a look in her eyes that made Wayne wince. What a perfect little actress! But there seemed just a chance that this was not deceit. For an instant he wavered, held back by subtle, finer intuition; then he beat down the mounting influence of truth in those dark-blue eyes, and spoke deliberately:

"The other thing is—if I win the game—a kiss."

Dorothy Huling's face flamed scarlet. But this did not affect Wayne so deeply, though it showed him his mistake, as the darkening shadow of disappointment in her eyes. If she had been a flirt, she would have been prepared for rudeness. He began casting about in his mind for some apology, some mitigation of his offense; but as he was about to speak, the sudden fading of her color, leaving her pale, and the look in her proud, dark eyes disconcerted him out of utterance.

"Certainly, Mr. Wayne. I agree to your price if you win the game."

But how immeasurable was the distance between the shy consent to wear Yale blue, and the pale, surprised agreement to his second proposal! Wayne experienced a strange sensation of personal loss.

While he endeavored to find his tongue, Miss Huling spoke to one of the boys standing near, and he started off on a run for the field. Presently Huling and the other players broke for the car, soon surrounding it in breathless anticipation.

"Wayne, is it straight? You'll pitch for us tomorrow?" demanded the captain, with shining eyes.

"Surely I will. Bellville don't need me. They've got Mackay, of Georgetown," replied Wayne.

Accustomed as he was to being mobbed by enthusiastic students and admiring friends, Wayne could not but feel extreme embarrassment at the reception accorded

him now. He felt that he was sailing under false colors.
The boys mauled him, the girls fluttered about him with
glad laughter. He had to tear himself away; and when he
finally reached his hotel, he went to his room, with his
mind in a tumult.

Wayne cursed himself roundly; then he fell into deep
thought. He began to hope he could retrieve the blunder.
He would win the game; he would explain to her the
truth; he would ask for an opportunity to prove he was
worthy of her friendship; he would not mention the kiss.
This last thought called up the soft curve of her red lips
and that it was possible for him to kiss her made the
temptation strong.

His sleep that night was not peaceful and dreamless.
He awakened late, had breakfast sent to his room, and
then took a long walk out into the country. After lunch
he dodged the crowd in the hotel lobby, and hurried up-
stairs, where he put on his baseball suit. The first person
he met upon going down was Reed, the Bellville man.

"What's this I hear, Wayne, about your pitching for
Salisbury today? I got your telegram."

"Straight goods," replied Wayne.

"But I thought you intended to pitch for us?"

"I didn't promise, did I?"

"No. Still, it looks fishy to me."

"You've got Mackay, haven't you?"

"Yes. The truth is, I intended to use you both."

"Well, I'll try to win for Salisbury. Hope there's no
hard feeling."

"Not at all. Only if I didn't have the Georgetown
crack, I'd yell murder. As it is, we'll trim Salisbury anyway."

"Maybe," answered Wayne, laughing. "It's a hot day,
and my arm feels good."

When Wayne reached the ball grounds, he thought
he had never seen a more inspiring sight. The bright green

oval was surrounded by a glittering mass of white and blue and black. Out along the foul lines were carriages, motors, and tally-hos, brilliant with waving fans and flags. Over the field murmured the low hum of many voices.

"Here you are!" cried Huling, making a grab for Wayne. "Where were you this morning? We couldn't find you. Come! We've got a minute before the practice whistle blows, and I promised to exhibit you."

He hustled Wayne down the first-base line, past the cheering crowd, out among the motors, to the same touring car that he remembered. A bevy of white-gowned girls rose like a covey of ptarmigans, and whirled flags of maroon and gray.

Dorothy Huling wore a bow of Yale blue upon her breast, and Wayne saw it and her face through a blur.

"Hurry, girls; get it over. We've got to practice," said the captain.

In the merry melee someone tied a knot of ribbon upon Wayne. Who it was he did not know: he saw only the averted face of Dorothy Huling. And as he returned to the field with a dull pang, he determined he would make her indifference disappear with the gladness of a victory for her team.

The practice was short, but long enough for Wayne to locate the glaring weakness of Salisbury at shortstop and third base. In fact, most of the players of his team showed rather poor form; they were overstrained, and plainly lacked experience necessary for steadiness in an important game.

Burns, the catcher, however, gave Wayne confidence. he was a short, sturdy youngster, with all the earmarks of a coming star. Huling, the captain, handled himself well at first base. The Bellville players were more matured, and some of them were former college cracks. Wayne saw that he had his work cut out for him.

The whistle blew. The Bellville team trotted to their

position in the field; the umpire called play, and tossed a ball to Mackay, the long, lean Georgetown pitcher.

Wells, the first batter, fouled out; Stamford hit an easy bounce to the pitcher, and Clews put up a little Texas leaguer—all going out, one, two, three, on three pitched balls.

The teams changed from bat to field. Wayne faced the plate amid vociferous cheering. He felt that he could beat this team even without good support. He was in the finest condition, and his arm had been resting for ten days. He knew that if he had control of his high inshoot, these Bellville players would feel the whiz of some speed under their chins.

He struck Moore out, retired Reed on a measly fly, and made Clark hit a weak grounder to second; and he walked in to the bench assured of the outcome. On some days he had poor control; on others his drop ball refused to work properly; but, as luck would have it, he had never had greater speed or accuracy, or a more bewildering fast curve than on this day, when he meant to win a game for a girl.

"Boys, I've got everything," he said to his fellow-players, calling them around him. "A couple of runs will win for us. Now, listen, I know Mackay. He hasn't any speed, or much of a curve. All he's got is a teasing slow ball and a foxy head. Don't be too anxious to hit. Make him put 'em over."

But the Salisbury players were not proof against the tempting slow balls that Mackay delivered. They hit at wide curves far off the plate, and when they did connect with the ball it was only to send an easy chance to the infielders.

The game seesawed along, inning after inning; it was a pitcher's battle that looked as if the first run scored would win the game. Mackay toyed with the Salisbury boys; it was his pleasure to toss up twisting, floating balls that could scarcely be hit out of the diamond. Wayne had the Bellville players utterly at his mercy; he mixed up his high jump and fast drop so cleverly, with his sweeping out-curve, that his opponents were unable to gauge his delivery at all.

In the first of the seventh, Barr for Bellville hit a ball which the third baseman should have fielded. But he fumbled. The second batter sent a fly to shortstop, who muffed it. The third hitter reached his base on another error by an infielder. Here the bases were crowded, and the situation had become critical all in a moment. Wayne believed the infield would go to pieces, and lose the game, then and there, if another hit went to short or third.

"Steady up, boys," called Wayne, and beckoned for his catcher.

"Burns, it's up to you and me," he said, in a low tone. "I've got to fan the rest of these hitters. You're doing splendidly. Now, watch close for my drop. Be ready to go down on your knees. When I let myself out, the ball generally hits the ground just back of the plate."

"Speed 'em over!" said Burns, his sweaty face grim and determined. "I'll get in front of 'em."

The head of the batting list was up for Bellville, and the whole Bellville contingent on the sidelines rose and yelled and cheered.

Moore was a left-handed hitter, who choked his bat up short, and poked at the ball. He was a good bunter, and swift on his feet. Wayne had taken his measure, as he had that of the other players, earlier in the game; and he knew it was good pitching to keep the ball in close to Moore's hands, so that if he did hit it, the chances were it would not go safe.

Summoning all his strength, Wayne took his long swing and shot the ball over the inside corner with terrific speed.

One strike!

Wayne knew it would not do to waste any balls if he wished to maintain that speed, so he put the second one in the same place. Moore struck too late.

Two strikes!

Then Burns signed for the last drop. Wayne delivered it with trepidation, for it was a hard curve to handle. Moore fell all over himself trying to hit it. Little Burns dropped to his knees to block the vicious curve. It struck the ground, and, glancing, boomed deep on the breast protector.

How the Salisbury supporters roared their approval! One man out—the bases full—with Reed, the slugging captain, at bat!

If Reed had a weakness, Wayne had not discovered it yet, although Reed had not hit safely. The captain stood somewhat back from the plate, a fact that induced Wayne to try him with the speedy outcurve. Reed lunged with a powerful swing, pulling away from the plate, and he missed the curve by a foot.

Wayne did not need to know any more. Reed had made his reputation slugging straight balls from heedless pitchers. He chopped the air twice more, and flung his bat savagely to the ground.

"Two out—play the hitter!" called Wayne to his team.

Clark, the third man up, was the surest batter on the Bellville team. He looked dangerous. He had made the only hit so far to the credit of his team. Wayne tried to work him on a high, fast ball close in. Clark swung freely and cracked a ripping liner to left. Half the crowd roared, and then groaned, for the beautiful hit went foul by several yards. Wayne wisely decided to risk all on his fast drop. Clark missed the first, fouled the second.

Two strikes!

Then he waited. He coolly let one, two, three of the fast drops go by without attempting to hit them. Burns valiantly got his body in front of them. These balls were all over the plate, but too low to be called strikes. With two strikes, and three balls, and the bases full, Clark had the advantage.

Tight as the place was, Wayne did not flinch. The game depended practically upon the next ball delivered. Wayne craftily and daringly decided to use another fast drop, for of all his assortment that would be the one least expected by Clark. But it must be started higher, so that in case Clark made no effort to swing, it would still be a strike.

Gripping the ball with a clinched hand, Wayne swung sharply, and drove it home with the limit of his power. It sped like a bullet, waist high, and just before reaching the plate darted downward, as if it had glanced on an invisible barrier.

Clark was fooled completely and struck futilely. But the ball caromed from the hard ground, hit Burns with a resounding thud, and bounced away. Clark broke for first, and Moore dashed for home. Like a tiger the little catcher pounced upon the ball, and, leaping back into line, blocked the sliding Moore three feet from the plate.

Pandemonium burst loose among the Salisbury adherents. The men bawled, the women screamed, the boys shrieked, and all waved their hats and flags, and jumped up and down, and manifested symptoms of baseball insanity.

In the first of the eighth inning, Mackay sailed up the balls like balloons, and disposed of three batters on the same old weak hits to his clever fielders. In the last of the eighth, Wayne struck out three more Bellville players.

"Burns, you're up," said Wayne, who, in his earnestness to win, kept cheering his comrades. "Do something. Get your base any way you can. Get in front of one. We must score this inning."

Faithful, battered Burns cunningly imposed his hip

over the plate and received another bruise in the interests of his team. The opposing players furiously stormed at the umpire for giving him his base, but Burns' trick went through. Burnett bunted skillfully, sending Burns to second. Cole hit a fly to center. Then Huling singled between short and third.

It became necessary for the umpire to delay the game while he put the madly leaping boys back off the coaching lines. The shrill, hilarious cheering gradually died out, and the field settled into a forced quiet.

Wayne hurried up to the plate and took his position. He had always been a timely hitter, and he gritted his teeth in his resolve to settle this game. Mackay whirled his long arm, wheeled, took his long stride, and pitched a slow, tantalizing ball that seemed never to get anywhere. But Wayne waited, timed it perfectly, and met it squarely.

The ball flew safely over short, and but for a fine sprint and stop by the left fielder, would have resulted in a triple, possibly a home run. As it was, Burns and Huling scored; and Wayne, by a slide, reached second base. When he arose and saw the disorderly riot, and heard the noise of that well-dressed audience, he had a moment of exultation. Then Wells flew out to center ending the chances for more runs.

As Wayne received the ball in the pitcher's box, he paused and looked out across the field toward a white-crowned motor car, and he caught a gleam of Dorothy Huling's golden hair, and wondered if she were glad.

For nothing short of the miraculous could snatch this game from him now. Burns had withstood a severe pounding, but he would last out the inning, and Wayne did not take into account the rest of the team. He opened up with no slackening of his terrific speed, and he struck out the three remaining batters on eleven pitched balls. Then in the rising din he ran for Burns and gave him a mighty hug.

"You made the gamest stand of any catcher I ever pitched to," he said warmly.

Burns looked at his quivering, puffed, and bleeding hands, and smiled as if to say that this was praise to remember, and reward enough. Then the crowd swooped down on them, and they were swallowed up in the clamor and surge of victory. When Wayne got out of the thick and press of it, he made a beeline for his hotel, and by running a gauntlet managed to escape.

Resting, dressing, and dining were matters which he went through mechanically, with his mind ever on one thing. Later, he found a dark corner of the porch and sat there waiting, thinking. There was to be a dance given in honor of the team that evening at the hotel. He watched the boys and girls pass up the steps. When the music commenced, he arose and went into the hall. It was bright with white gowns, and gay with movement.

"There he is. Grab him, somebody," yelled Huling.

"Do something for me, quick," implored Wayne of the captain, as he saw the young people wave toward him.

"Salisbury is yours tonight," replied Huling.

"Ask your sister to save me one dance."

Then he gave himself up. He took his mead of praise and flattery, and he withstood the battery of arch eyes modestly, as became the winner of many fields. But even the reception after the Princeton game paled in comparison with this impromptu dance.

She was here. Always it seemed, while he listened or talked or danced, his eyes were drawn to a slender, graceful form, and a fair face crowned with golden hair. Then he was making his way to where she stood near one of the open windows.

He never knew what he said to her, nor what reply she made, but she put her arm in his, and presently they were gliding over the polished floor. To Wayne the dance was a dream. He led her through the hall and out upon the balcony, where composure strangely came to him.

"Mr. Wayne, I have to thank you for saving the day for us. You pitched magnificently."

"I would have broken my arm to win that game," burst out Wayne. "Miss Huling, I made a blunder yesterday. I thought there was a conspiracy to persuade me to throw down Bellville. I've known of such things, and I resented it. You understand what I thought. I humbly offer my apologies, and beg that you forget the rude obligation I forced upon you."

How cold she was! How unattainable in that moment! He caught his breath, and rushed on.

"Your brother and the management of the club have asked me to pitch for Salisbury the remainder of the season. I shall be happy to—if—"

"If what?" She was all alive now, flushing warmly, dark eyes alight, the girl of his dreams.

"If you will forgive me—if you will let me be your friend—if—Miss Huling, you will again wear that bit of Yale blue."

"If, Mr. Wayne, you had very sharp eyes you would have noticed that I still wear it!"

The Manager of
Madden's Hill

WILLIE HOWARTH loved baseball. He loved it all the
more because he was a cripple. The game was
more beautiful and wonderful to him because he would
never be able to play it. For Willie had been born with
one leg shorter than the other; he could not run and at 11
years of age it was all he could do to walk with a crutch.

Nevertheless Willie knew more about baseball than
any other boy on Madden's Hill. An uncle of his had once
been a ballplayer and he had taught Willie the fine points
of the game. And this uncle's ballplayer friends, who occasionally visited him, had imparted to Willie the vernacular of the game. So that Willie's knowledge of players
and play, and particularly of the strange talk, the wild and
whirling words on the lips of the real baseball men, made
him the envy of every boy on Madden's Hill, and a mine
of information. Willie never missed attending the games
played on the lots, and he could tell why they were won
or lost.

Willie suffered considerable pain, mostly at night, and
this had given him a habit of lying awake in the dark
hours, grieving over that crooked leg that forever shut
him out of the heritage of youth. He had kept his secret

well; he was accounted shy because he was quiet and had never been able to mingle with the boys in their activity. No one except his mother dreamed of the fire and hunger and pain within his breast. His schoolmates called him "Daddy." It was a name given for his bent shoulders, his labored gait, and his thoughtful face, too old for his years. And no one, not even his mother, guessed how that name hurt Willie.

It was a source of growing unhappiness with Willie that the Madden's Hill boys were always beaten by the other teams of the town. He really came to lose his sadness over his own misfortune in pondering on the wretched play of the Madden's Hill baseball club. He had all a boy's pride in the locality where he lived. And when the Bogg's Farm team administered a crushing defeat to Madden's Hill, Willie grew desperate.

Monday he met Lane Griffith, the captain of the Madden's Hill nine.

"Hello, Daddy," said Lane. He was a big, aggressive boy, and in a way had a fondness for Willie.

"Lane, you got an orful trimmin' up on the Boggs. What'd you wanter let them country jakes beat you for?"

"Aw, Daddy, they was lucky. Umpire had hayseed in his eyes! Robbed us! He couldn't see straight. We'll trim them down here Saturday."

"No, you won't—not without team work. Lane, you've got to have a manager."

"Durn it! Where're we goin' to get one?" Lane blurted out.

"You can sign me. I can't play, but I know the game. Let me coach the boys."

The idea seemed to strike Captain Griffith favorably. He prevailed upon all the boys living on Madden's Hill to come out for practice after school. Then he presented them to the managing coach. The boys were inclined to poke fun at Daddy Howarth and ridicule him; but the idea was a novel one and they were in such a state of subjection from many beatings that they welcomed any change. Willie sat on a bench improvised from a soapbox and put them through a drill of batting and fielding. The next day in his coaching he included bunting and sliding. He played his men in different positions and for three more days he drove them unmercifully.

When Saturday came, the day for the game with Bogg's Farm, a wild protest went up from the boys. Willie experienced his first bitterness as a manager. Out of forty aspirants for the Madden's Hill team he could choose but nine to play the game. And as a conscientious manager he could use no favorites. Willie picked the best players and assigned them to positions that, in his judgment, were the best suited to them. Bob Irvine wanted to play first base and he was down for right field. Sam Wickhart thought he was the fastest fielder, and Willie had him slated to catch. Tom Lindsay's feelings were hurt because he was not to play in the infield. Eddie Curtis suffered a fall in pride when he discovered he was not down to play second base. Jake Thomas, Tay Tay Mohler, and Brick Grace all wanted to pitch. The manager had chosen Frank Price for that important position, and Frank's one ambition was to be a shortstop.

So there was a deadlock. For a while there seemed no possibility of a game. Willie sat on the bench, the center of a crowd of discontented, quarreling boys. Some were jealous, some were outraged, some tried to pacify and persuade the others. All were noisy. Lane Griffith stood by his manager and stoutly declared the players should play the positions to which they had been assigned or not at all. And he was entering into a hot argument with Tom Lindsay when the Bogg's Farm team arrogantly put in an appearance.

The way that team from the country walked out upon the field made a great difference. The spirit of

Madden's Hill roused to battle. The game began swiftly and went on wildly. It ended almost before the Hill boys realized it had commenced. They did not know how they had won but they gave Daddy Howarth credit for it. They had a bonfire that night to celebrate the victory and they talked baseball until their parents became alarmed and hunted them up.

Madden's Hill practiced all that next week and on Saturday beat the Seventh Ward team. In four more weeks they had added half a dozen more victories to their record. Their reputation went abroad. They got uniforms, and baseball shoes with spikes, and bats and balls, and gloves. They got a mask, but Sam Wickhart refused to catch with it.

"Sam, one of these days you'll be stoppin' a high in-shoot with your eye," sagely remarked Daddy Howarth. "An' then where'll I get a catcher for the Natchez game?"

Natchez was the one name on the lips of every Madden's Hill boy. For Natchez had the great team of the town and, roused by the growing repute of the Hill club, had condescended to arrange a game. When that game was scheduled for July Fourth Daddy Howarth set to driving his men. Early and late he had them out. This manager, in keeping with all other famous managers, believed that batting was the thing which won games. He developed a hard-hitting team. He kept everlastingly at them to hit and run, hit and run.

On the Saturday before the Fourth, Madden's Hill had a game to play that did not worry Daddy and he left his team in charge of the captain.

"Fellers, I'm goin' down to the Round House to see Natchez play. I'll size up their game," said Daddy.

When he returned he was glad to find that his team had won its ninth straight victory, but he was not communicative in regard to the playing of the Natchez club. He appeared more than usually thoughtful.

The Fourth fell on Tuesday. Daddy had the boys out Monday and he let them take only a short, sharp practice. Then he sent them home. In his own mind, Daddy did not have much hope of beating Natchez. He had been greatly impressed by their playing, and one inning toward the close of the Round House game they had astonished him with the way they suddenly seemed to break loose and deluge their opponents in a flood of hits and runs. He could not understand this streak of theirs—for they did the same thing every time they played—and he was too good a baseball student to call it luck.

He had never wanted anything in his life, not even to have two good legs, as much as he wanted to beat Natchez. For the Madden's Hill boys had come to believe him infallible. He was their idol. They imagined they had only to hit and run, to fight and never give up, and Daddy would make them win. There was not a boy on the team who believed that Natchez had a chance. They had grown proud and tenacious of their dearly won reputation. First of all, Daddy thought of his team and their loyalty to him; then he thought of the glory lately come to Madden's Hill, and lastly of what it meant to him to have risen from a lonely watcher of the game—a cripple who could not even carry a bat—to manager of the famous Hill team. It might go hard with the boys to lose this game, but it would break his heart.

From time out of mind there had always been rivalry between Madden's Hill and Natchez. And there is no rivalry so bitter as that between boys. So Daddy, as he lay awake at night planning the system of play he wanted to use, left out of all account any possibility of a peaceful game. It was comforting to think that if it came to a fight Sam and Lane could hold their own with Bo Stranathan and Slugger Blandy.

In the managing of his players Daddy observed strict discipline. It was no unusual thing for him to fine them.

On practice days and off the field they implicitly obeyed him. During actual play, however, they had evinced a tendency to jump over the traces. It had been his order for them not to report at the field Tuesday until 2 o'clock. He found it extremely difficult to curb his own inclination to start before the set time. And only the stern duty of a man to be an example to his players kept Daddy at home.

He lived near the ball grounds, yet on this day, as he hobbled along on his crutch, he thought the distance interminably long, and for the first time in weeks the old sickening resentment at his useless leg knocked at his heart. Manfully Daddy refused admittance to that old gloomy visitor. He found comfort and forgetfulness in the thought that no strong and swift-legged boy of his acquaintance could do what he could do.

Upon arriving at the field Daddy was amazed to see such a large crowd. It appeared that all the boys and girls in the whole town were in attendance, and, besides, there was a sprinkling of grown-up people interspersed here and there around the diamond. Applause greeted Daddy's appearance and members of his team escorted him to the soapbox bench.

Daddy cast a sharp eye over the Natchez players practicing on the field. Bo Stranathan had out his strongest team. They were not a prepossessing nine. They wore soiled uniforms that did not match in cut or color. But they pranced and swaggered and strutted! They were boastful and boisterous. It was a trial for any Madden's Hill boy just to watch them.

"Wot a swelled bunch!" exclaimed Tom Lindsay.

"Fellers, if Slugger Blandy tries to pull any stunt on me today he'll get a swelleder nut," growled Lane Griffith.

"T-t-t-t-t-te-te-tell him t-t-t-to keep out of m-m-m-my way an' not b-b-b-b-bl-block me," stuttered Tay Tay Mohler.

"We're a-goin' to skin 'em," said Eddie Curtis.

"Cheese it, you kids, till we git in the game," ordered Daddy. "Now, Madden's Hill, hang round an' listen. I had to sign articles with Natchez—had to let them have their umpire. So we're up against it. But we'll hit this pitcher Muckle Harris. He ain't got any steam. An' he ain't got much nerve. Now every feller who goes up to bat wants to talk to Muck. Call him a big swelled stiff. Tell him he can't break a pane of glass—tell him he can't put one over the pan—tell him if he does you'll slam it down in the sand bank. Bluff the whole team. Keep scrappy all the time. See! That's my game today. This Natchez bunch needs to be gone after. Holler at the umpire. Act like you want to fight."

Then Daddy sent his men out for practice.

"Boss, enny ground rules?" inquired Bo Stranathan. He was a big, bushy-haired boy with a grin and protruding teeth. "How many bases on wild throws over first base an' hits over the sand bank?"

"All you can get," replied Daddy, with a magnanimous wave of hand.

"Huh! Lemmee see your ball?"

Daddy produced the ball that he and Lane had made for the game.

"Huh! Watcher think? We ain't goin' to play with no mush ball like thet," protested Bo. "We play with a hard ball. Looka here! We'll trow up the ball."

Daddy remembered what he had heard about the singular generosity of the Natchez team to supply the balls for the games they played.

"We don't hev to pay nothin' fer them balls. A man down at the Round House makes them for us. They ain't no balls as good," explained Bo, with pride.

However, as Bo did not appear eager to pass over the balls for examination Daddy simply reached out and took them. They were small, perfectly round and as hard as bullets. They had no covers. The yarn had been closely and tightly wrapped and then stitched over with fine beeswaxed thread. Daddy fancied he detected a difference in the weight of the ball, but Bo took them back before Daddy could be sure of that point.

"You don't have to fan about it. I know a ball when I see one," observed Daddy. "But we're on our own grounds an' we'll use our own ball. Thanks all the same to you, Stranathan."

"Huh! All I gotta say is we'll play with my ball er there won't be no game," said Bo suddenly.

Daddy shrewdly eyed the Natchez captain. Bo did not look like a fellow wearing himself thin from generosity. It struck Daddy that Bo's habit of supplying the ball for the game might have some relation to the fact that he always carried along his own umpire. There was a strange feature about this umpire business and it was that Bo's man had earned a reputation for being particularly fair. No boy ever had any real reason to object to Umpire Gale's decisions. When Gale umpired away from the Natchez grounds his close decisions always favored the other team, rather than his own. It all made Daddy keen and thoughtful.

"Stranathan, up here on Madden's Hill we know how to treat visitors. We'll play with your ball. . . . Now keep your gang of rooters from crowdin' on the diamond."

"Boss, it's your grounds. Fire 'em off if they don't suit you. . . . Come on, let's git in the game. Watcher want—field er bat?"

"Field," replied Daddy briefly.

Billy Gale called "Play," and the game began with Slugger Blandy at bat. The formidable way in which he swung his club did not appear to have any effect on Frank Price or the player back of him. Frank's most successful pitch was a slow, tantalizing curve, and he used it. Blandy lunged at the ball, missed it and grunted.

"Frank, you got his alley," called Lane.

Slugger fouled the next one high in the air back of the plate. Sam Wickhart, the stocky bowlegged catcher, was a fiend for running after foul flies, and now he plunged into the crowd of boys, knocking them right and left, and he caught the ball. Whisner came up and hit safely over Griffith, whereupon the Natchez supporters began to howl. Kelly sent a grounder to Grace at short stop. Daddy's weak player made a poor throw to first base, so the runner was safe. Then Bo Stranathan batted a stinging ball through the infield, scoring Whisner.

"Play the batter! Play the batter!" sharply called Daddy from the bench.

Then Frank struck out Molloy and retired Dundon on an easy fly.

"Fellers, git in the game now," ordered Daddy, as his players eagerly trotted in. "Say things to that Muckle Harris! We'll walk through this game like sand through a sieve."

Bob Irvin ran to the plate waving his bat at Harris.

"Put one over, you freckleface! I've been dyin' fer this chanst. You're on Madden's Hill now."

Muckle evidently was not the kind of pitcher to stand coolly under such bantering. Obviously he was not used to it. His face grew red and his hair waved up. Swinging hard, he threw the ball straight at Bob's head. Quick as a cat, Bob dropped flat.

"Never touched me!" he chirped, jumping up and pounding the plate with his bat. "You couldn't hit a barn door. Come on. I'll paste one a mile!"

Bob did not get an opportunity to hit, for Harris could not locate the plate and passed him to first on four balls.

"Dump the first one," whispered Daddy in Grace's ear. Then he gave Bob a signal to run on the first pitch.

Grace tried to bunt the first ball, but he missed it. His attempt, however, was so violent that he fell over in front of the catcher, who could not recover in time to throw, and Bob got to second base. At this juncture, the Madden's Hill band of loyal supporters opened up with a mingling of shrill yells and whistles and jangling of tin cans filled with pebbles. Grace hit the next ball into second base and, while he was being thrown out, Bob raced to third. With Sam Wickhart up it looked good for a score, and the crowd yelled louder. Sam was awkward yet efficient, and he batted a long fly to right field. The fielder muffed the ball. Bob scored, Sam reached second base, and the crowd yelled still louder. Then Lane struck out and Mohler hit to shortstop, retiring the side.

Natchez scored a run on a hit, a base on balls, and another error by Grace. Every time a ball went toward Grace at short Daddy groaned. In their half of the inning Madden's Hill made two runs, increasing the score 3 to 2.

The Madden's Hill boys began to show the strain of such a close contest. If Daddy had voiced aloud his fear it would have been: "They'll blow up in a minnit!" Frank Price alone was slow and cool, and he pitched in masterly style. Natchez could not beat him. On the other hand, Madden's Hill hit Muck Harris hard, but superb fielding kept runners off the bases. As Daddy's team became more tense and excited Bo Stranathan's players grew steadier and more arrogantly confident. Daddy saw it with distress, and he could not realize just where Natchez had license for such confidence. Daddy watched the game with the eyes of a hawk.

As the Natchez players trooped in for their sixth inning at bat, Daddy observed a marked change in their demeanor. Suddenly they seemed to have been let loose; they were like a band of Indians. Daddy saw everything. He did not miss seeing Umpire Gale take a ball from his pocket and toss it to Frank, and Daddy wondered if that was the ball which had been in the play. Straightway, however, he forgot that in the interest of the game.

Bo Stranathan bawled: "Wull, Injuns, hyar's were we do 'em. We've jest ben loafin' along. Git ready to tear the air, you rooters!"

Kelly hit a wonderfully swift ball through the infield. Bo batted out a single. Malloy got up in the way of one of Frank's pitches, and was passed to first base. Then, as the Natchez crowd opened up in shrill clamor, the impending disaster fell. Dundon hit a bounder down into the infield. The ball appeared to be endowed with life. It bounded low, then high and, cracking into Grace's hands, bounced out and rolled away. The runners raced around the bases.

Pickens sent up a tremendous fly, the highest ever batted on Madden's Hill. It went over Tom Lindsay in center field, and Tom ran and ran. The ball went so far up that Tom had time to cover the ground, but he could not judge it. He ran round in a little circle, with hands up in bewilderment. And when the ball dropped it hit him on the head and bounded away.

"Run, you Injun, run!" bawled Bo. "What'd I tell you? We ain't got 'em goin', oh, no! Hittin' 'em on the head!"

Bill dropped a slow, teasing ball down the third-base line. Jake Thomas ran desperately for it, and the ball appeared to strike his hands and run up his arms and caress his nose and wrap itself round his neck and then roll gently away. All the while, the Natchez runners tore wildly about the bases and the Natchez supporters screamed and whistled. Muck Harris could not bat, yet he hit the first ball and it shot like a bullet over the infield. Then Slugger Blandy came to the plate. The ball he sent out knocked Grace's leg from under him as if it were a tenpin. Whisner popped a fly over Tay Tay Mohler's head. Now Tay Tay was fat and slow, but he was a sure catch. He got under the ball. It struck his hands and jumped

back twenty feet up into the air. It was a strangely live
ball. Kelly again hit to shortstop, and the ball appeared to
start slow, to gather speed with every bound and at last to
dart low and shoot between Grace's legs.

"Haw! Haw!" roared Bo. "They've got a hole at
short. Hit fer the hole, fellers. Watch me! Jest watch me!"

And he swung hard on the first pitch. The ball
glanced like a streak straight at Grace, took a vicious
jump, and seemed to flirt with the infielder's hands, only
to evade them.

Malloy fouled a pitch and the ball hit Sam Wickhart
square over the eye. Sam's eye popped out and assumed
the proportions and color of a huge plum.

"Hey!" yelled Blandy, the rival catcher. "Air you
ketchin' with yer mug?"

Sam would not delay the game nor would he don the
mask.

Daddy sat hunched on his soapbox, and, as in a hate-
ful dream, he saw his famous team go to pieces. He put
his hands over his ears to shut out some of the uproar.
And he watched that little yarn ball fly and shoot and
bound and roll to crush his fondest hopes. Not one of his
players appeared able to hold it. And Grace had holes in
his hands and legs and body. The ball went right through
him. He might as well have been so much water. Instead
of being a shortstop he was simply a hole. After every hit
Daddy saw that ball more and more as something alive. It
sported with his infielders. It bounded like a huge jackrabbit, and went swifter and higher at every bound. It was
here, there, everywhere.

And it became an infernal ball. It became endowed
with a fiendish propensity to run up a player's leg and all
about him, as if trying to hide in his pocket. Grace's efforts
to find it were heartbreaking to watch. Every time it
bounded out to center field, which was of frequent occur-
rence, Tom would fall on it and hug it as if he were trying

to capture a fleeing squirrel. Tay Tay Mohler could stop the ball, but that was no great credit to him, for his hands took no part in the achievement. Tay Tay was fat and the ball seemed to like him. It boomed into his stomach and banged against his stout legs. When Tay saw it coming he dropped on his knees and valorously sacrificed his anatomy to the cause of the game.

Daddy tried not to notice the scoring of runs by his opponents. But he had to see them and he had to count. Ten runs were as ten blows! After that each run scored was like a stab in his heart. The play went on, a terrible fusilade of wicked ground balls that baffled any attempt to field them. Then, with nineteen runs scored, Natchez appeared to tire. Sam caught a foul fly, and Tay Tay, by obtruding his wide person to the path of infield hits, managed to stop them, and throw out the runners.

Score—Natchez, 21; Madden Hill, 3.

Daddy's boys slouched and limped wearily in.

"Wot kind of a ball s that?" panted Tom, as he showed his head with a bruise as large as a goose egg.

"T-t-t-t-ta-ta-tay-tay-tay-tay—" began Mohler, in great excitement, but as he could not finish what he wanted to say no one caught his meaning.

Daddy's watchful eye had never left that wonderful, infernal little yarn ball. Daddy was crushed under defeat, but his baseball brains still continued to work. He saw Umpire Gale leisurely step into the pitcher's box, and leisurely pick up the ball and start to make a motion to put it in his pocket.

Suddenly fire flashed all over Daddy.

"Hyar! Don't hide that ball!" he yelled, in his piercing tenor.

He jumped up quickly, forgetting his crutch, and fell headlong. Lane and Sam got him upright and handed the crutch to him. Daddy began to hobble out to the pitcher's box.

"Don't you hide that ball. See! I've got my eye on this game. That ball was in play, an' you can't use the other."

Umpire Gale looked sheepish, and his eyes did not meet Daddy's. Then Bo came trotting up.

"What's wrong, boss?" he asked.

"Aw, nuthin'. You're tryin' to switch balls on me. That's all. You can't pull off any stunts on Madden's Hill."

"Why, boss, thet ball's all right. What you hollerin' about?"

"Sure that ball's all right," replied Daddy. "It's a fine ball. An' we want a chanst to hit it! See?"

Bo flared up and tried to bluster, but Daddy cut him short.

"Give us our innin'—let us git a whack at that ball, or I'll run you off Madden's Hill."

Bo suddenly looked a little pale and sick.

"Course youse can git a whack at it," he said, in a weak attempt to be natural and dignified.

Daddy tossed the ball to Harris, and as he hobbled off the field he heard Bo calling out low and cautiously to his players. Then Daddy was certain he had discovered a trick. He called his players around him.

"This game ain't over yet. It ain't any more'n begun. I'll tell you what. Last innin' Bo's umpire switched balls on us. That ball was lively. An' they tried to switch back on me. But nix! We're goin' to git a chanst to hit that lively ball. An' they're goin' to git a dose of their own medicine. Now, you dead ones—come back to life! Show me some hittin' an' runnin'."

"Daddy, you mean they run in a trick on us?" demanded Lane, with flashing eyes.

"Funny about Natchez's strong finishes!" replied Daddy, coolly, as he eyed his angry players.

They let out a roar, and then ran for the bats.

The crowd, quick to sense what was in the air,

thronged to the diamond and manifested alarming signs of outbreak.

Sam Wickhart leaped to the plate and brandished his club.

"Sam, let him pitch a couple," called Daddy from the bench. "Mebbe we'll git wise then."

Harris had pitched only twice when the fact became plain that he could not throw this ball with the same speed as the other. The ball was heavier; besides Harris was also growing tired. The next pitch Sam hit far out over the center fielder's head for a home run. It was a longer hit than any Madden's Hill boy had ever made. The crowd shrieked its delight. Sam crossed the plate and then fell on the bench beside Daddy.

"Say! that ball nearly knocked the bat out of my hands," panted Sam. "It made the bat spring!"

"Fellers, don't wait," ordered Daddy. "Don't give the umpire a chanst to roast us now. Slam the first ball!"

The aggressive captain lined the ball at Bo Stranathan. The Natchez shortstop had a fine opportunity to make the catch, but he made an inglorious muff. Tay Tay hurried to bat. Umpire Gale called the first pitch a strike. Tay slammed down his club. "T-t-t-t-to-to-twasn't over," he cried. "T-t-t-tay—"

"Shut up," yelled Daddy. "We want to git this game over today."

Tay Tay was fat and he was also strong, so that when beef and muscle both went hard against the ball it traveled. It looked as if it were going a mile straight up. All the infielders ran to get under it. They got into a tangle, into which the ball descended. No one caught it, and thereupon the Natchez players began to rail at one another. Bo stormed at them, and they talked back to him. Then when Tom Lindsay hit a little slow grounder into the infield it seemed that a just retribution had overtaken the great Natchez team.

Ordinarily this grounder of Tom's would have been easy for a novice to field. But this peculiar grounder, after it has hit the ground once, seemed to wake up and feel lively. It lost its leisurely action and began to have celerity. When it reached Dundon it had the strange, jerky speed so characteristic of the grounders that had confused the Madden's Hill team. Dundon got his hands on the ball and it would not stay in them. When finally he trapped it Tom had crossed first base and another runner had scored. Eddie Curtis cracked another at Bo. The Natchez captain dove for it, made a good stop, bounced after the rolling ball, and then threw to Kelly at first. The ball knocked Kelly's hands apart as if they had been paper. Jake Thomas batted left handed and he swung hard on a slow pitch and sent the ball far into right field. Runners scored. Jake's hit was a three-bagger. Then Frank Price hit up an infield fly. Bo yelled for Dundon to take it and Dundon yelled for Harris. They were all afraid to try for it. It dropped safely while Jake ran home.

With the heavy batters up the excitement increased. A continuous scream and incessant rattle of tin cans made it impossible to hear what the umpire called out. But that was not important, for he seldom had a chance to call either ball or strike. Harris had lost his speed and nearly every ball he pitched was hit by the Madden's Hill boys. Irvine cracked one down between short and third. Bo and Pickens ran for it and collided while the ball jauntily skipped out to left field and, deftly evading Bell, went on and on. Bob reached third. Grace hit another at Dundon, who appeared actually to stop it four times before he could pick it up, and then he was too late. The doughty bow-legged Sam, with his huge black eye, hung over the plate and howled at Muckle. In the din no one heard what he said, but evidently Muck divined it. For he roused to the spirit of a pitcher who would die of shame if he could not fool a one-eyed batter. But Sam swooped down and upon the first ball and drove it back toward the pitcher. Muck could not get out of the way and the ball made his leg buckle under him. Then that hit glanced off to begin a marvelous exhibition of high and erratic bounding about the infield.

Daddy hunched over his soapbox bench and hugged himself. He was farsighted and he saw victory. Again he watched the queer antics of that little yarn ball, but now with different feelings. Every hit seemed to lift him to the skies. He kept silent, though every time the ball fooled a Natchez player Daddy wanted to yell. And when it started for Bo and, as if in revenge, bounded wickeder at every bounce to skip off the grass and make Bo look ridiculous, then Daddy experienced the happiest moments of his baseball career. Every time a tally crossed the plate he would chalk it down on his soapbox.

But when Madden's Hill scored the nineteenth run without a player being put out, then Daddy lost count. He gave himself up to revel. He sat motionless and silent; nevertheless his whole internal being was in the state of wild tumult. It was as if he was being rewarded in joy for all the misery he had suffered because he was a cripple. He could never play baseball, but he had baseball brains. He had been too wise for the tricky Stranathan. He was the coach and manager and general of the great Madden's Hill nine. If ever he had to lie awake at night again he would not mourn over his lameness; he would have something to think about. To him would be given the glory of beating the invincible Natchez team. So Daddy felt the last bitterness leave him. And he watched that strange little yarn ball, with its wonderful skips and darts and curves. The longer the game progressed and the wearier Harris grew, the harder the Madden's Hill boys batted the ball and the crazier it bounced at Bo and his sick players. Finally, Tay Tay Mohler hit a teasing grounder down to Bo.

Then it was as if the ball, realizing a climax, made ready for a final spurt. When Bo reached for the ball it was somewhere else. Dundon could not locate it. And Kelly, rushing down to the chase, fell all over himself and his teammates trying to grasp the illusive ball, and all the time Tay Tay was running. He never stopped. But as he was heavy and fat he did not make fast time on the bases. Frantically the outfielders ran in to head off the bouncing ball, and when they had succeeded Tay Tay had performed the remarkable feat of making a home run on a ball batted into the infield.

That broke Natchez's spirit. They quit. They hurried for their bats. Only Bo remained behind a moment to try to get his yarn ball. But Sam had pounced upon it and given it safely to Daddy. Bo made one sullen demand for it.

"Funny about them fast finishes of yours!" said Daddy scornfully. "Say! the ball's our'n. The winnin' team gits the ball. Go home an' look up the rules of the game!"

Bo slouched off the field to a shrill hooting and tin canning.

"Fellers, what was the score?" asked Daddy.

Nobody knew the exact number of runs made by Madden's Hill.

"Gimme a knife, somebody," said the manager.

When it had been produced Daddy laid down the yarn ball and cut into it. The blade entered readily for an inch and then stopped. Daddy cut all around the ball, and removed the cover of tightly wrapped yarn. Inside was a solid ball of India rubber.

"Say! it ain't so funny now—how that ball bounced," remarked Daddy.

"Wot you think of that!" exclaimed Tom, feeling the lump on his head.

"T-t-t-t-t-t-t-ta-tr—" began Tay Tay Mohler.

"Say it! Say it!" interrupted Daddy.

"Ta-ta-ta-tr-trimmed them wa-wa-wa-wa-with their own b-b-b-b-b-ba-ba-ball," finished Tay.

Old Well-Well

H E bought a ticket at the 25-cent window, and edging his huge bulk through the turnstile, laboriously followed the noisy crowd toward the bleachers. I could not have been mistaken. He was Old Well-Well, famous from Boston to Baltimore as the greatest baseball fan in the East. His singular yell had pealed into the ears of five hundred thousand worshippers of the national game and would never be forgotten.

At sight of him I recalled a friend's baseball talk. "You remember Old Well-Well? He's all in—dying, poor old fellow! It seems young Burt, whom the Phillies are trying out this spring, is Old Well-Well's nephew and protege. Used to play on the Murray Hill team; a speedy youngster. When the Philadelphia team was here last, Manager Crestline announced his intention to play Burt in center field. Old Well-Well was too ill to see the lad get his try-out. He was heartbroken and said: 'If I could only see one more game!' "

The recollection of this random baseball gossip and the fact that Philadelphia was scheduled to play New York that very day, gave me a sudden desire to see the game with Old Well-Well. I did not know him, but where on

earth were introductions as superfluous as on the bleachers? It was a very easy matter to catch up with him. He
walked slowly, leaning hard on a cane and his wide
shoulders sagged as he puffed along. I was about to make
some pleasant remark concerning the prospects of a fine
game, when the sight of his face shocked me and I drew
back. If ever I had seen shadow of pain and shade of
death they hovered darkly around Old Well-Well.

No one accompanied him; no one seemed to recog-
nize him. The majority of that merry crowd of boys and
men would have jumped up wild with pleasure to hear
his well-remembered yell. Not much longer than a year
before, I had seen ten thousand fans rise as one man and
roar a greeting to him that shook the stands. So I was
confronted by a situation strikingly calculated to rouse my
curiosity and sympathy.

He found an end seat on a row at about the middle of
the right-field bleachers and I chose one across the aisle
and somewhat behind him. No players were yet in sight.
The stands were filling up and streams of men were filing
into the aisles of the bleachers and piling over the
benches. Old Well-Well settled himself comfortably in his
seat and gazed about him with animation. There had
come a change to his massive features. The hard lines had
softened; the patches of gray were no longer visible; his
cheeks were ruddy; something akin to a smile shone on
his face as he looked around, missing no detail of the familiar scene.

During the practice of the home team Old Well-Well
sat still with his big hands on his knees; but when the
gong rang for the Phillies, he grew restless, squirming in
his seat and half rose several times. I divined the impor-
tuning of his old habit to greet his team with the yell that
had made him famous. I expected him to get up; I waited
for it. Gradually, however, he became quiet as a man gov-

erned by severe self-restraint and directed his attention to
the Philadelphia center fielder.

At a glance I saw that the player was new to me and
answered the newspaper description of young Burt. What
a lively looking athlete! He was tall, lithe, yet sturdy. He
did not need to chase more than two fly balls to win me.
His graceful, fast style reminded me of the great Curt
Welch. Old Well-Well's face wore a rapt expression. I discovered myself hoping Burt would make good; wishing
he would rip the boards off the fence; praying he would
break up the game.

It was Saturday, and by the time the gong sounded
for the game to begin the grandstand and bleachers were
packed. The scene was glittering, colorful, a delight to the
eye. Around the circle of bright faces rippled a low, merry
murmur. The umpire, grotesquely padded in front by his
chest protector, announced the batteries, dusted the plate,
and throwing out a white ball, sang the open sesame of
the game: "Play!"

Then Old Well-Well arose as if pushed from his seat
by some strong propelling force. It had been his wont always when play was ordered or in a moment of silent
suspense, or a lull in the applause, or a dramatic pause
when hearts beat high and lips were mute, to bawl out
over the listening, waiting multitude his terrific blast:
"Well-Well-Well!"

Twice he opened his mouth, gurgled and choked, and
then resumed his seat with a very red, agitated face;
something had deterred him from his purpose, or he had
been physically incapable of yelling.

The game opened with White's sharp bounder to the
infield. Wesley had three strikes called on him, and Kelly
fouled out to third base. The Phillies did no better, being
retired in one, two, three order. The second inning was
short and no tallies were chalked up. Brain hit safely in
the third and went to second on a sacrifice. The bleachers

began to stamp and cheer. He reached third on an infield hit that the Philadelphia shortstop knocked down but could not cover in time to catch either runner. The cheer in the grandstand was drowned by the roar in the bleachers. Brain scored on a fly-ball to left. A double along the right foul line brought the second runner home. Following that the next batter went out on strikes.

In the Philadelphia half of the inning young Burt was the first man up. He stood left-handed at the plate and looked formidable. Duveen, the wary old pitcher for New York, to whom this new player was an unknown quantity, eyed his easy position as if reckoning on a possible weakness. Then he took his swing and threw the ball. Burt never moved a muscle and the umpire called strike. The next was a ball, the next a strike; still Burt had not moved.

"Somebody wake him up!" yelled a wag in the bleachers. "He's from Slumbertown, all right, all right!" shouted another.

Duveen sent up another ball, high and swift. Burt hit straight over the first baseman, a line drive that struck the front of the right-field bleachers.

"Peacherino!" howled a fan.

Here the promise of Burt's speed was fulfilled. Run! He was fleet as a deer. He cut through first like the wind, settled to a driving stride, rounded second, and by a good, long slide beat the throw in to third. The crowd, who went to games to see long hits and daring runs, gave him a generous handclapping.

Old Well-Well appeared on the verge of apoplexy. His ruddy face turned purple, then black; he rose in his seat; he gave vent to smothered gasps; then he straightened up and clutched his hands into his knees.

Burt scored his run on a hit to deep short, an infielder's choice, with the chances against retiring a runner at the plate. Philadelphia could not tally again that inning.

New York blanked in the first of the next. For their opponents, an error, a close decision at second favoring the runner, and a single to right tied the score. Bell of New York got a clean hit in the opening of the fifth. With no one out and chances for a run, the impatient fans let loose. Four subway trains in collision would not have equalled the yell and stamp in the bleachers. Maloney was next to bat and he essayed a bunt. This the fans derided with hoots and hisses. No teamwork, no inside ball for them.

"Hit it out!" yelled a hundred in unison.

"Home run!" screamed a worshipper of long hits.

As if actuated by the sentiments of his admirers Maloney lined the ball over short. It looked good for a double; it certainly would advance Bell to third; maybe home. But no one calculated on Burt. His fleetness enabled him to head the bounding ball. He picked it up cleanly, and checking his headlong run, threw toward third base. Bell was half way there. The ball shot straight and low with terrific force and beat the runner to the bag.

"What a great arm!" I exclaimed, deep in my throat. "It's the lad's day! He can't be stopped."

The keen newsboy sitting below us broke the amazed silence in the bleachers.

"Wot d'ye tink o' that?"

Old Well-Well writhed in his seat. To him it was a one-man game, as it had come to be for me. I thrilled with him; I gloried in the making good of his protege; it got to be an effort on my part to look at the old man, so keenly did his emotion communicate itself to me.

The game went on, a close, exciting, brilliantly fought battle. Both pitchers were at their best. The batters batted out long flies, low liners, and sharp grounders; the fielders fielded these difficult chances without misplay. Opportunities came for runs, but no runs were scored for several innings. Hopes were raised to the highest pitch only to be dashed astonishingly away. The crowd in the grandstand swayed to every pitched ball; the bleachers tossed like surf in a storm.

To start the eighth, Stranathan of New York tripled along the left foul line. Thunder burst from the fans and rolled swellingly around the field. Before the hoarse yelling, the shrill hooting, the hollow stamping had ceased Stranathan made home on an infield hit. Then bedlam broke loose. It calmed down quickly, for the fans sensed trouble between Binghamton, who had been thrown out in the play, and the umpire who was waving him back to the bench.

"You dizzy-eyed old woman, you can't see straight!" called Binghamton.

The umpire's reply was lost, but it was evident that the offending player had been ordered out of the grounds.

Binghamton swaggered along the bleachers while the umpire slowly returned to his post. The fans took exception to the player's objection and were not slow in expressing it. Various witty enconiums, not to be misunderstood, attested to the bleachers' love of fair play and their disgust at a player's getting himself put out of the game at a critical stage.

The game proceeded. A second batter had been thrown out. Then two hits in succession looked good for another run. White, the next batter, sent a single over second base. Burt scooped the ball on the first bounce and let drive for the plate. It was another extraordinary throw. Whether ball or runner reached home base first was most difficult to decide. The umpire made his sweeping wave of hand and the breathless crowd caught his decision.

"Out!"

In action and sound the circle of bleachers resembled a long curved beach with a mounting breaker thundering turbulently high.

"Rob—b—ber—r!" bawled the outraged fans, betraying their marvelous inconsistency.

Old Well-Well breathed hard. Again the wrestling of his body signified an inward strife. I began to feel sure that the man was in a mingled torment of joy and pain, that he fought the maddening desire to yell because he knew he had not the strength to stand it. Surely, in all the years of his long following of baseball he had never had the incentive to express himself in his peculiar way that rioted him now. Surely, before the game ended he would split the winds with his wonderful yell.

Duveen's only base on balls, with the help of a bunt, a steal, and a scratch hit, resulted in a run for Philadelphia, again tying the score. How the fans raged at Fuller for failing to field the lucky scratch.

"We had the game on ice!" one cried.

"Get him a basket!"

New York men got on bases in the ninth and made strenuous efforts to cross the plate, but it was not to be. Philadelphia opened up with two scorching hits and then a double steal. Burt came up with runners on second and third. Half the crowd cheered in fair appreciation of the way fate was starring the ambitious young outfielder; the other half, dyed-in-the-wool home-team fans, bent forward in a waiting silent gloom of fear. Burt knocked the dirt out of his spikes and faced Duveen. The second ball pitched he met fairly and it rang like a bell.

No one in the stands saw where it went. But they heard the crack, saw the New York shortstop stagger and then pounce forward to pick up the ball and speed it toward the plate. The catcher was quick to tag the incoming runner, and then snap the ball to first base, completing a double play.

When the crowd fully grasped this, which was after an instant of bewilderment, a hoarse crashing roar rolled out across the field to bellow back in loud echo from Coogan's Bluff. The grandstand resembled a colored corn field waving in a violent wind; the bleachers lost all semblance of anything. Frenzied, flinging action—wild chaos— shrieking cries—manifested sheer insanity of joy.

When the noise subsided, one fan, evidently a little longer-winded than his comrades, cried out hysterically: "O-h! I don't care what becomes of me—now-w!"

Score tied, three to three, game must go ten innings —that was the shibboleth; that was the overmastering truth. The game did go ten innings—eleven—twelve, every one marked by masterly pitching, full of magnificent catches, stops and throws, replete with reckless base-running and slides like flashes in the dust. But they were unproductive of runs. Three to three! Thirteen innings!

"Unlucky thirteenth," wailed a superstitious fan.

I had got down to plugging, and for the first time, not for my home team. I wanted Philadelphia to win, because Burt was on the team. With Old Well-Well sitting there so rigid in his seat, so obsessed by the playing of the lad, I turned traitor to New York.

White cut a high twisting bounder inside the third base, and before the ball could be returned he stood safely on second. The fans howled with what husky voice they had left. The second hitter batted a tremendously high fly toward center field. Burt wheeled with the crack of the ball and raced for the ropes. Onward the ball soared like a sailing swallow; the fleet fielder ran with his back to the stands. What an age that ball stayed in the air! Then it lost its speed, gracefully curved and began to fall. Burt lunged forward and upwards; the ball lit in his hands and stuck there as he plunged over the ropes into the crowd. White had leisurely trotted half way to third; he saw the catch, ran back to touch second and then easily made third on the throw-in. The applause that greeted Burt proved the splendid spirit of the game. Bell placed a safe little hit over short, scoring White. Heaving, bobbing bleachers—wild, broken, roar on roar!

Score four to three—only one half inning left for Philadelphia to play—now the fans rooted for another run! A swift double-play, however, ended the inning.

Philadelphia's first hitter had three strikes called on him.

"Asleep at the switch!" yelled a delighted fan.

The next batter went out on a weak pop-up fly to second.

"Nothin' to it!"

"Oh, I hate to take this money!"

"All-l o-over!"

Two men at least of all that vast assemblage had not given up victory for Philadelphia. I had not dared to look at Old Well-Well for a long while. I dreaded the next portentious moment. I felt deep within me something like clairvoyant force, an intangible belief fostered by hope.

Magoon, the slugger of the Phillies, slugged one against the left-field bleachers, but, being heavy and slow, he could not get beyond second base. Cless swung with all his might at the first pitched ball, and instead of hitting it a mile as he had tried, he scratched a mean, slow, teasing grounder down the third-base line. It was as safe as if it had been shot out of a cannon. Magoon went to third.

The crowd suddenly awoke to ominous possibilities: sharp commands came from the players' bench. The Philadelphia team was bowling and hopping on the side lines, and had to be put down by the umpire.

An inbreathing silence fell upon stands and field, quiet, like a lull before a storm.

When I saw young Burt start for the plate and realized it was his turn at bat, I jumped as if I had been shot. Putting my hand on Old Well-Well's shoulder I whispered: "Burt's at bat: He'll break up this game! I know he's going to lose one!"

The old fellow did not feel my touch; he did not hear my voice; he was gazing toward the field with an expression on his face to which no human speech could render justice. He knew what was coming. It could not be denied him in that moment.

How confidently young Burt stood up to the plate! None except a natural hitter could have had his position. He might have been Wagner for all he showed of the tight suspense of that crisis. Yet there was a tense alert poise to his head and shoulders which proved he was alive to his opportunity.

Duveen plainly showed he was tired. Twice he shook his head to his catcher, as if he did not want to pitch a certain kind of ball. He had to use extra motion to get his old speed, and he delivered a high straight ball that Burt fouled over the grandstand. The second ball met a similar fate. All the time the crowd maintained that strange waiting silence. The umpire threw out a glistening white ball, which Duveen rubbed in the dust and spat upon. Then he wound himself up into a knot, slowly unwound, and swinging with effort, threw for the plate.

Burt's lithe shoulders swung powerfully. The meeting of ball and bat fairly cracked. The low driving hit lined over second a rising glittering streak, and went far beyond the center fielder.

Bleachers and stands uttered one short cry, almost a groan, and then stared at the speeding runners. For an instant, approaching doom could not have been more dreaded. Magoon scored. Cless was rounding second when the ball lit. If Burt was running swiftly when he turned first he had only got started, for then his long sprinter's stride lengthened and quickened. At second he was flying; beyond second he seemed to merge into a gray flitting shadow.

I gripped my seat strangling the uproar within me. Where was the applause? The fans were silent, choked as

I was, but from a different cause. Cless crossed the plate
with the score that defeated New York; still the tension
never laxed until Burt beat the ball home in as beautiful a
run as ever thrilled an audience.

In the bleak dead pause of amazed disappointment
Old Well-Well lifted his hulking figure and loomed, towered over the bleachers. His wide shoulders spread, his
broad chest expanded, his breath whistled as he drew it
in. One fleeting instant his transfigured face shone with a
glorious light. Then, as he threw back his head and
opened his lips, his face turned purple, the muscles of his
cheeks and jaw rippled and strung, the veins on his fore-
head swelled into bulging ridges. Even the back of his
neck grew red.

"Well!—Well!—Well!!!"

Ear-splitting stentorian blast! For a moment I was
deafened. But I heard the echo ringing from the cliff, a
pealing clarion call, beautiful and wonderful, winding
away in hollow reverberation, then breaking out anew
from building to building in clear concatenation.

A sea of faces whirled in the direction of that long
unheard yell. Burt had stopped statue-like as if stricken in
his tracks; then he came running, darting among the spectators who had leaped the fence.

Old Well-Well stood a moment with slow glance lin-
gering on the tumult of emptying bleachers, on the
moving mingling colors in the grandstand, across the
green field to the gray-clad players. He staggered forward
and fell.

Before I could move, a noisy crowd swarmed about
him, some solicitous, many facetious. Young Burt leaped
the fence and forced his way into the circle. Then they
were carrying the old man down to the field and toward
the clubhouse.

I waited until the bleachers and field were empty.
When I finally went out there was a crowd at the gate

surrounding an ambulance. I caught a glimpse of Old Well-Well. He lay white and still, but his eyes were open, smiling intently. Young Burt hung over him with a pale and agitated face. Then a bell clanged and the ambulance clattered away.